Learning the Ropes . . .

"Where do you come from?" asked the boy with the hood. Sipho told them he had set off that morning from the township.

"What made you come?" asked the army-jacket boy.

"It's bad there," said Sipho. "I can't stay at my home."

They didn't seem surprised by what he said.

"I need to earn money. Is it hard?" he asked.

"It's best by Checkers. When you push *amatrolley* for the shoppers they give you money or they give you something to eat," said the boy with the hood.

"Sometimes they give you nothing and you can starve," said the other abruptly. Tilting his head back, he looked at Sipho through half-closed eyes and added, "Do you like to eat cats?"

BEVERLEY
NAIDOO

NO TURNING BACK

—

A Novel of
South
Africa

HarperTrophy®
A Division of HarperCollinsPublishers

No Turning Back
A Novel of South Africa
Copyright © 1995 by Beverley Naidoo
First published by the Penguin Group, London, England.
All rights reserved. No part of this book may be used
or reproduced in any manner whatsoever without
written permission except in the case of brief quotations
embodied in critical articles and reviews. Printed in the
United States of America. For information address
HarperCollins Children's Books,
a division of HarperCollins Publishers,
10 East 53rd Street, New York, NY 10022.

Library of Congress Cataloging-in-Publication Data
Naidoo, Beverley.
No turning back : a novel of South Africa / Beverley Naidoo.
p.   cm.
Summary: When the abuse at home becomes too much for twelve-year-old
Sipho, he runs away to the streets of Johannesburg and learns to survive in
the post-apartheid world.
ISBN 0-06-027505-7. — ISBN 0-06-027506-5 (lib. bdg.)
ISBN 0-06-440749-7 (pbk.)
[1. Street children—Fiction.   2. South Africa—Fiction.   3. Blacks—South
Africa—Fiction.]   I. Title.
PZ7.N1384No   1997   96-28980
[Fic]—dc20   CIP
                                                                  AC

Typography by Tom Starace and Michele N. Tupper
❖
First Harper Trophy edition, 1999

Visit us on the World Wide Web!
http://www.harperchildrens.com

*For Maya and Praveen, born in exile, and the
children of the new South Africa*

Contents

Acknowledgments

I owe special thanks to a number of people from
Street-Wise in Johannesburg: Jill Swart-Kruger,
whose research with street children was invaluable; Knox Mogashoa, shelter manager; Nomfundo
Gwaai, care worker; Webster Nhlanhla Nxele, assistant care worker; and the children themselves for
their openness during workshops. Special thanks are
also due to Martha Mokgoko, director of the Speak
Barefoot Teacher Training Project in Alexandra, and
to the Barefoot Teachers for all their insights both at
the beginning and final stages of this work. I thank
Pippa Stein, Department of Applied Language
Studies at the University of the Witwatersrand, for
her help. I thank most warmly my colleague and
comrade Olusola Oyeleye for her collaboration in the
workshops that preceded my work on the novel. My
thanks also go to the many young people who commented so perceptively on the novel at the final draft
stage, including Sibi Madlingozi, Louise Gerardy,
Jongisa Klaas, Zipho Nonganga, Deepa Daya, Saleha
Seedat, Leigh van den Berg, and Kathy Hansford, and

their teacher Lesley Foster from Collegiate Junior School for Girls, Port Elizabeth, South Africa, and all the 1994 Standard Fives and their teacher Michael Phillips from Orange Grove Primary School, Johannesburg; as well as Ben Holman, Emily Whitehouse, David Myhill and Rosa Bransky in England and Aidin Carey from Boston. My thanks go to Rosemary Stones at Viking Children's Books for her encouragement, and finally I wish to thank my daughter, Maya, my first reader, and my husband, Nandha, our wonderful cook.

A Gift from God
Being a Street Child

What is this gift doing on the street?
Where does this gift sleep?
He sleeps on the street or on the bed like you?
What does this child eat?

This child has a dream but because
he is on the street
he cannot make his dream come true.
He is now using drugs to forget who he is.
What is he doing with his life?
What future does his life on the street have for him?

When the nights come
he has to see where is he going to sleep.
He must drug himself
so that he can pretend he is inside the house
like you
going to sleep on his bed with his warm blankets.

That's only imagination.
The truth is he is going to sleep on the street

And all that strong wind and rain will end up on him.

When he suffers from all these pains—
Who is looking after him
Who is taking care of him
or to the doctor?
He has to wait until he gets better on his own.

These children are people like us.
Let us help them.
They are a gift from God.
Put them first.

> —*Webster Nhlanhla Nxele*
> *Street-Wise, Johannesburg*

Note: I would like to offer special thanks to Webster Nhlanhla Nxele for providing this poem. With experience of life on the streets himself, he has been working as an assistant care worker at the Street-Wise shelter for homeless children in Johannesburg.

No Turning Back

1. Runaway

Tiptoeing toward his mother's bed, Sipho touched the table to steady himself. He held his breath and glanced at the sleeping figures. Two gray shapes that could stir at any time. A small square of plastic above the bed let in the dim early-morning light. His mother lay near the edge, one hand resting over her rounded stomach. His stepfather was snoring heavily, a giant of a man stretched across the bed. Each snore shook the stillness of the tiny room. But it was a sigh from his mother that almost made him drop her bag and leave empty-handed. Then his fingers touched the coins. Grasping them, he turned and silently fled. Past the chipped wooden table, the kerosene stove and the pot of cold porridge from the night before. Past his mattress on the floor with the crumpled blanket. Past the orange-crate cupboard and out the door. He eased it shut, praying that the snoring would cover the sound of creaking hinges.

And then he ran. Keeping his head down, he weaved his way through the patchwork of shacks in the smoky half-light, hoping against hope that no one would call his name. Thin chinks of yellow light and the smell of kerosene lamps behind the sheets of iron and wooden planks showed that people were beginning to rise. Ma and "him" would have been getting up by now if they had had work to go to. Sipho's heart was thumping against his chest. It had been screwed up for the last few days, like the rest of his insides, as tight as a fist. But now it was going wild like the tail of a puppy just let out of a cage. He would have to get it under control before he got to the taxi rank.

Coming out from the shacks, he sprinted past the shop boarded up overnight. He could be seen more easily here. The quickest way would be to cut across by the men's hostel. But that was dangerous. Bullets whistling between the great grim building and the houses nearby had brought death to many people. No one knew when the fighting would start again, and Ma had forbidden him to go near the place.

"That bullet won't stop to ask who you are," Ma had said. But why should he listen to what Ma said anymore? Still, it was safer to go the long way around, past his school.

Squares of misty light from houses on each

side lit the way, and high above him, electric strips shone dully through the smoke. There were other people on the road already, most walking in the same direction. Sipho slowed down to a half-jog, half-walk. He might draw too much attention to himself if he ran. Passing the crisscross wire fencing around the school, he shifted to the other side of the road. Even though the gate was locked, he could imagine the head teacher suddenly appearing from the low redbrick building and wanting to know where he was going.

The taxi rank was already humming with the early-morning crowd milling alongside a line of minibuses. Pavement sellers had already set up their stalls. Some people in the lines carried bags and boxes, perhaps of things to sell in town themselves. With so many taxis, he had to make sure he got in the right one. Glancing briefly at a row of faces, he noticed a woman looking at him. She had a baby on her back and seemed about Ma's age. No, he wouldn't ask her. Instead he moved away and asked a young man which was the right line for Hillbrow.

"Take any one for Jo'burg city center. It's that side." The man pointed to where the crowd was thicker.

Slipping behind a line of people, Sipho was pleased he had managed to ask the question so smoothly. If only everyone would move along quickly so he could get inside the taxi. He kept his eyes trained in the direction of the school. What if Ma had waked up? She wouldn't feel up to coming after him, but she would wake his stepfather. If Ma sent him out looking for Sipho, he would be raging mad—even without a drink. Sipho could just imagine him storming through the crowd, shouting Sipho's name, demanding to know if anyone had seen a small boy age twelve . . . a boy with big ears, the kind you can get hold of.

Sipho shivered, pulled his woolen cap down lower and clasped his arms around him. It was cold. He should have put on two sweaters. But he hadn't really been thinking clearly for the last few days. Ever since the last beating. He didn't know whether to forgive Ma or not. If she didn't want him nearly killed, why did she complain so much about him to his stepfather? She knew his terrible temper. And all because Sipho had come in late. He had explained it was an accident. When his friend Gordon had met him outside the shop and asked if he wanted to watch TV, he had been happy. He had only intended to go for a short while. Gordon's mother was out working late, and no one reminded him about the time. One movie had led to another. Sipho had quite forgotten Ma waiting for him. Ma lying on the bed on her own in the shack because his stepfather stayed out drinking. Ma crying often. Yes, Ma had definitely become more tense since she had been forced to give up her job because of the baby. And Ma changing, changed everything.

The line moved in fits and starts. He willed it to hurry up. *Shesha! Shesha!* Shifting his gaze between the taxis and the road by the school, Sipho watched anxiously as each one filled up and veered off. He was between a man in a smock and an elderly woman carrying a large plastic bag. The bag bumped into Sipho's legs from time to time, but the old lady didn't seem to notice as she talked with the lady behind her.

"It was at this very place the man was shot. He was standing right where I am standing now. I was just there by the taxi."

"Hey! This place is too dangerous," the other replied.

Sipho stared hard at the ground around his feet. Was that slightly darker patch remains of a man's blood?

"Come on, young man. This taxi can't wait all day!"

Propelled forward to the open door, Sipho climbed aboard.

Wedged tightly between the man in a blue smock and another man, he found himself sitting opposite the old lady with the bag. As the taxi lurched on its way, Sipho felt her eyes on him. He tried to avoid looking back. She reminded him of Gogo, his grandmother, whose eyes had always been able to bore into him. There was nothing he could hide from Gogo. She had understood everything. Like the way she had known how much he had wanted the little black puppy and had got the white farmer to sell it to her cheap. But that was all in the past now, before Gogo had died. Gogo dying was really the beginning of the trouble. Ma had come to collect him from the farm in the valley of green hills to stay with her near Johannesburg.

It was a long day's journey in the bus. The green hills were left far behind as the land turned to brown, with the road like a gray rope stretching endlessly ahead of them. On the way, Ma had told him about Johannesburg—the big buildings, the lights and the shops—and he had been excited. It was night by the time they approached the city center. From the bus, the city had looked magical. As if thousands upon thousands of stars had fallen to the earth and were spread out in front of them. Traveling out to the township by taxi, he could only catch glimpses of the brightly lit shop windows. Ma had promised that one day, when she got leave from her work, she would bring Sipho into town.

"What's that, Ma?" he had asked, pointing to

a cluster of lights glittering high up above all the rest. They lit up what seemed to be a giant drum with enormous round saucer eyes looking out at the black sky.

"That one is the Hillbrow tower," Ma had said.

Gazing up before it passed from view, he felt a little awed by its strangeness.

But when they had left the lights behind and arrived at the township, outside the city, everything was very different. Even that would have been all right. But why hadn't Ma told him anything about his stepfather until they were stumbling in the dark, hand in hand, through the shacks? The gigantic figure whose head almost touched the roof had come as a total shock. "So this is the one you've been crying about" was all he had said, hardly even glancing at Sipho. Roughly throwing open the door, he had bent down and stormed out. Ma had sat Sipho down and tried to talk to him, but her words had whirled over his head. Later that night, on his mattress by the door, Sipho had been awakened by a terrible banging, swearing and shouting. It was his stepfather returning, and Ma was trying to calm him down. Sipho had tried to shut out the noise by covering his head with the blanket.

That was more than six months ago, and although he had been out of the township with

Ma to go to the supermarket, he had not yet been into the city itself. Ma had lost her job before she could keep her promise. Now here he was speeding down a highway, entering Johannesburg on his own. With the old lady's eyes looking into him, his heart was starting its wild puppydog nonsense again, and he had to find a way of calming it down.

2. Hillbrow

BP . . . SHELL . . . HONDA . . . COCA-COLA . . . Signs in front of garages and great boxlike metal, brick and concrete buildings flashed by on either side. Stretching his neck, Sipho saw people milling through gates and doorways. It reminded him of when Ma was working. Her pay from working at the café hadn't been much, but with payday every Friday, his stepfather wasn't always so angry then. As long as he got his beer money. Even so, they had argued. Like when Ma needed extra money for Sipho's school uniform. But the really bad rows started when Ma got big with the baby and the café owner sacked her. Then there was no more regular money on Fridays. Perhaps if she had still been working, he wouldn't have been running away now . . .

Suddenly the driver swerved and swore as another taxi pulled out in front of them. The passengers bumped against each other, and the old lady opposite was jolted into talking.

"Why is there still so much fighting, my children? We see death every day."

He was relieved that the old lady's gaze had shifted away from him. She was the oldest person there and seemed to be talking to no one in particular.

"It's very true, Mama," answered the man in the blue smock. "There's nowhere safe nowadays."

"My head is too old to understand all this," the old lady continued, shaking her head. "Why is brother killing brother?"

His mother used those exact words too. Brother killing brother.

A smart-looking woman in a black suit with a small brown case on her lap turned to the old lady. "Let's hope the elections will bring us peace, Mama. When everyone makes their cross on the paper, there should be no need for fighting anymore."

The old lady sighed heavily, her face so creased with deep lines that it looked to Sipho like bark on a very old tree.

"Did you hear what Mr. Mandela said on TV last night?" asked the man in the blue smock.

"He talks like a president even now," said a voice from the row behind.

As more people joined in, Sipho only half listened. He needed to see where he was going. The garages and factories had given way to a mixture of shops and houses of different shapes and sizes. There were no shacks here. The early-morning sun shone on bright white walls and red roofs of houses, all with gardens and pavements between them and the tarmac streets. Not like the township, where lots of houses and shacks spilled right onto the dusty, stony roads. Springing up ahead, a mass of buildings reached upward to the sky. One was taller and slimmer than all the others. Sipho recognized the concrete drum with the saucer eyes. The tower slipped from view, and Sipho's fingers tightened their grip on his seat.

"Short left! Hillbrow!"

The man who had taken Sipho's fare signaled to him. The taxi jerked and whined as the driver pulled in to the left. Trying not to step on feet or packages, Sipho squeezed his way out of the taxi. He could feel the old lady's eyes on his back. The sliding door wasn't even closed behind him before the vehicle was hurtling off on its way to the city center.

Standing at the corner where he had alighted, he tried to take in where he was. Traffic was coming from all directions, and the smell of gasoline was almost overpowering. Didn't Gogo speak about good country air, saying that town air had poison? Perhaps this was what she had meant.

"Move over!"

A large hand pushed him roughly to one side. "You'll make us late for work!"

Another taxi had pulled up at the corner, with people clambering out. Within seconds it had swung back out into the road. Sipho looked around to see which way he should go. It could be any way. Apart from a garage opposite him, all around were tall buildings with the sun glinting in glass windows high above. The streets were lined with shops, and street sellers were setting up stalls along the pavement. Close by, a woman sitting on a blanket was laying out plastic plates with an orange, apple and banana on each. In between were small piles of sweets. Feeling in his pocket, he pulled out the remaining coins. Ma's purse had been filled with coins that weren't worth much. There was a one-rand coin, which he put back in his pocket. Offering all the others, which came to ninety-seven cents, he was allowed to take one of the piles.

Unwrapping the sweet, which was brightest red, Sipho savored its cherry flavor. Why not go down this street? There was no need to hurry now. Where would he hurry to? No one knew him, and he knew no one. All he knew was what his friend Gordon had told him. Children lived on the streets here. Gordon had been to Hillbrow and seen them asking for money and doing jobs. That way they got something to eat. Well, if they could do it, so could he. And if he was lucky, some of them might be friendly too.

He walked slowly, examining the shop windows on the way. In a furniture shop he gazed at a mattress marked R475. Almost 500 rand just for a mattress! Ma had struggled to find twenty rand to buy his old one from the man who sold goods from his cart. Behind the mattress was a chest of drawers marked R600. This place was expensive. At home they used cardboard boxes for their clothes. Next door at the shoe shop, Sipho gave up checking the prices and just studied the designs. Would those white kung fu shoes fit him, he wondered? He could picture himself in a full kung fu outfit. Imagine if he was the strongest boy in the world! His stepfather would never dare to hit him then.

These shops were quite different from the local township ones, where everything was stuffed together into one small place. Nearly every shop here had something different . . . clothes . . . electrical things . . . medicines . . . even a shop just for books. But it was a window full of cameras that held the best surprises. The lenses stared out at Sipho like detectives behind dark glasses. If only Gordon was here! He knew a lot about cameras because his uncle was a photographer. Sometimes the two of them pretended to take funny shots of each other. What if they had that camera with the long fat lens? Trying to imagine what it would be like to hold, as if he was a real photographer, he stepped backward, not noticing the body that lay near the shop entrance under a blanket.

"You blerry fool!"

The body propped itself up as Sipho almost tripped over it. To his amazement, under the blanket and a mop of bushy, matted hair was a man with a red, heavily bearded face! It was definitely a white man.

"Why don't you blerry look where you're going?" the man growled.

Backing away and saying "Sorry," Sipho quickly walked on, but then turned back to look again. The man was clutching his blanket and rolling over. Lots of black people had nowhere to sleep, but didn't all white people have houses? Gordon had talked about *malunde*, boys like him, who were street children. He hadn't said anything about white people sleeping on the streets.

From the other side of the road, in big red letters, a sign beamed out FUN AND GAMES! Although he could see the place was barred up, Sipho crossed the road and tried to peer through the bars. Inside, it was dark, but he could make out that there were machines with blinking lights.

"Do you like those kind of games?" said a voice.

Looking up, Sipho saw a white man with a pale face and a black mustache smiling at him. The man was laying out shirts and jeans on a table in front of the next-door shop. Not sure what to say, Sipho nodded.

"You must be careful you don't spend all your money on them!" warned the man, whose mustache hung down a little below each side of his mouth.

Sipho nodded again. The man didn't sound angry, but he sounded like a teacher. That could mean trouble. Although Sipho wanted to look longer at the machines, he turned and set off quickly.

The streets were filling up with people. Waiting for the traffic lights to turn green, Sipho took note of the cars passing by. Some were very sleek and shiny. Like the shimmering pale blue Benz turning the corner, which suddenly pulled up in the next block. As if from nowhere, two boys of about Sipho's age appeared, one on the pavement, the other in the road, and began directing the driver into a parking space. They whirled their hands and pointed as the car moved backward and forward, finally coming to a halt. Crossing the road, Sipho stopped nearby and watched as a lady with light brown hair tumbling around her face got out of the car. She ignored the boy on the pavement, who had raised the palm of his hand. He wore an old gray track top with a hood covering his head.

"I'll do the meter myself," she said.

Carefully she studied the writing on the machine by the road before putting in her coins, turning and clicking the metal key after each one. Finally she fumbled in her bag and placed a coin in the hands of the boy with the hood.

"See you look after it nicely," she said, sweeping a glance at both boys before swinging her bag over her shoulder and hurrying off down the road.

The boy with the coin showed it to the other. It looked like ten cents from where Sipho stood. He was wondering if he should speak to them, when the boy who had been in the road came toward him. He was the larger of the two and was wearing what looked like an oversized brown army jacket. His nose was running a little, and he used his sleeve to wipe it.

"I see you've been watching us," he said. His voice was rather low and rough.

"*Heyta, buti*!" Sipho offered his greeting a little nervously. "I'm new in this place."

"Where do you come from?" asked the boy with the hood. Sipho told them he had set off that morning from the township.

"What made you come?" asked the army-jacket boy.

"It's bad there," said Sipho. "I can't stay at my home."

He didn't say how he had taken the money from his mother's purse. He wanted to forget that, and they didn't ask. But they didn't seem surprised by what he said.

"I need to earn money. Is it hard?" he asked.

"It's best by Checkers. When you push *ama-trolley* for the shoppers they give you money or they give you something to eat," said the boy with the hood.

"Sometimes they give you nothing and you can starve," said the other abruptly.

Tilting his head back, he looked at Sipho through half-closed eyes and added, "Do you like to eat cats?"

Taken aback by this question, Sipho made a face.

"Don't worry. He's only joking," giggled the boy with the hood. He turned to his friend.

"Hey, Joseph, it must be you that's eating cats! You finished all the cats in Soweto and now you want to start in Hillbrow!"

Joseph swung out his arm to catch the boy

with the hood, but he was already out of reach, calling out to Sipho to follow.

"We'll take you to Checkers. Then you can see for yourself how it is!"

3. First Earnings

⬦⬦⬦⬦⬦

*J*abu, the boy with the hood, said that Checkers wasn't far. Sipho offered his sweets. Jabu immediately popped one into his mouth, but Joseph pocketed his, taking out a small cigarette stump instead, which he lit. He inhaled vigorously a couple of times, letting out the smoke through his nose, before offering the *stompie* to Sipho. Still sucking his sweet, Sipho shook his head. He did smoke occasionally with Gordon, even though it made him cough.

Whenever a sports car passed them, Jabu called out its name or a comment. He seemed to know the makes of all the cars. When a red open-top BMW passed them, he whistled so loudly that the passengers turned and looked at him, half frowning, half amused.

"Be My Wife!" Jabu shouted behind them.

Grinning, he continued chattering about cars . . . which was fastest, which was the best and which he would like. Although Joseph sometimes joined in, Sipho noticed that he was quieter and not so ready to smile as Jabu.

A loose collection of boys was spread out near the supermarket. A couple stood outside a shop with bread and cakes in the window. When someone came out of the shop, each boy held out an open palm. Another boy was pushing a cart and another was loading boxes into a car. Two others were leaning against the glass front of the store, talking. Jabu led Sipho across to them. They seemed a bit older than the others, and the one on the left was very tall. He wore a red peaked cap, which he shifted slightly to one side over his narrow face as he looked at Sipho.

"This is Sipho," said Jabu. "It's his first day in Hillbrow. He was looking for Checkers."

The tall boy asked the same questions about where he had come from and why. When Sipho finished explaining, he just said, "That's okay." The boy next to him remained silent throughout. A scar ran down the side of his cheek, and his eyes were fixed on a spot just past Sipho's face. Sipho felt his stomach crimp a little.

Walking away, Jabu revealed that Lucas, the tall boy, was the leader in their gang. If Lucas agreed, Sipho could walk around and sleep with their group. Sipho looked worried.

"How will he choose?" he asked.

"He'll watch to see if you make trouble. If there are fights, he'll say you must go."

For a second Sipho felt his heart might begin its full puppy-tail thumping again. It would be scary, sleeping on the streets on your own. With others around it wouldn't be so bad. He wouldn't start any fights, but what if someone started a fight with him? Some of the boys looked a lot bigger than him. Jabu seemed to read his thoughts.

"You'll be fine with Lucas," he said. "But just watch out for Vusi, the one with the scar."

Before Sipho had time to ask what he meant, Jabu led the way inside the supermarket.

"Sometimes they chase us like dogs. But other times they let us right in."

He took Sipho toward a cash register. "Watch me," he whispered.

There were packers helping the customers load their carts at the cash registers. A lady was ready to leave, and Jabu moved forward.

"Ma'am?" he offered, putting a hand out toward the cart.

The lady shook her head with a frown, almost knocking him with the cart. Jabu jumped back. A man was next in the line. Sipho thought he too would dismiss Jabu, but instead he let the boy take the cart from him and push it out. Jabu winked across at Sipho as he left.

Sipho stood back for a minute, looking into

the shop. Here were white people, black people, everybody. It was like that outside, but suddenly, inside the shop, he noticed it more. In the township there were hardly any white people. Except, of course, for some of the police and soldiers. In their tanks, like monsters with evil eyes and mouths, he had seen them crashing through the township streets—even into people's yards. It had shocked him because on the farm with Gogo he had never seen such monstrous machines. When the police had come to the farm, it was always in a car or truck. There was always at least one white police officer who would lead the way into the house to talk in private with the white farmer. But it was never long before one of the house servants would slip out to warn Gogo and the other farm workers of the reason for the visit.

At one of the checkouts, a small fair-haired boy was crying to his mother that he wanted "sweeties." His face had the same kind of light brown freckles that reminded Sipho of Kobus, the farmer's son. He and Kobus had played together when they were smaller. Even when Sipho started working in the garden and doing jobs for the Missus, Kobus would come and hurry him to finish the work. They would run off to play soccer or climb trees by the dried-up waterfall. Sometimes they raced each other past the mealie fields along the stony paths up to a hideout they had made on a hill. Sitting together panting, they would look down at what was happening on the farmland below and plan their games for the hideout. But if Kobus's mother saw them, she would scold her son for stopping Sipho from doing his work properly. Then the time for playing got less. After the long walk back from the one-room school where he went with other workers' children, Sipho had to spend most afternoons working in the fields. Kobus was sent away to boarding school. When he came back they didn't play anymore, even on Sundays when Sipho didn't have to go to the fields.

Scanning the customers by the checkouts, Sipho saw that black and white were lining up together in whatever order they had arrived. That had never happened at the country store where Gogo bought provisions once a month. Whites didn't often go there, but if they did, they were always served first. Sometimes he had gone along with Kobus to buy sweets. The Indian shopkeeper would greet Kobus by name and ask him about his father and the family, while Sipho hovered by the door, hoping Kobus would choose some of his favorite sweets as well.

"Still here?"

Jabu was back already. Sipho grinned, feeling

a little sheepish. Caught dreaming! Just like at school!

"You have to move sharp if you want a job," said Jabu.

Jabu kept his eyes trained on the registers, and before long he was again in charge of a cart. Sipho gave himself a little shake, determined to follow Jabu's lead. The lady with the little boy who had been crying for sweets was paying and about to leave. The child, with a package of sweets in his hand, had slipped through the checkouts and was beginning to dart around the front of the shop.

"Robbie! Come back here!" his mother called sharply.

But the little boy took no notice, and as the mother let go of the cart to get him by the hand, Sipho stepped forward to take hold of the cart.

"All right! You can take it to the car for me," said the woman.

"I want to push the cart!" announced the little boy.

Sipho couldn't help smiling as the child eased himself out of his mother's grip and struggled to reach the handlebar. He pushed the cart slowly so the little boy didn't trip. The car was parked up the hill, and when they reached it Sipho helped unload the packages, then stood waiting by the cart as the mother put the child into the car, strapping him into a special seat. With her back to Sipho, she looked in her bag before turning around and holding out a twenty-cent coin.

"You were very helpful," she said with a smile.

Sipho bobbed slightly in thanks as she dropped the coin into his open palm. It wouldn't buy much, but it was the first coin he had earned in Hillbrow! He was learning fast! He didn't wait to see the car drive off, but quickly wheeled the cart back down the hill, ready to find another customer.

4. Empty Pockets

XXXIXXXIX

Two hours later, Sipho was both hot and hungry. He had been kept busy, although Jabu was much quicker at spotting likely customers. Sometimes he was given twenty cents, even a couple of fifties, but more often it was ten or five. One lady gave him two apples from her shopping. He stuffed one into each of his trouser pockets, with his woolen hat in one of them too, and looked around for Jabu. Perhaps they could break off and eat them. But at that moment a man with a tanned, leathery face and enormous square shoulders, wearing khaki shirt and trousers, indicated that he wanted Sipho to push his cart. It was filled to the brim and was heavy. The man strode ahead, leading the way to a truck at the top of the hill.

"Inside there!" He pointed to Sipho to unload.

Two sacks lay at the bottom of the cart—one of oranges and one of potatoes. Sipho struggled to lift them out, feeling the strain on his back and the sweat under his arms. When he had finished, he straightened himself and looked toward the khaki figure towering near him. Turning his back to Sipho, the man strolled to the front of the truck, opened the door and climbed into the driver's seat. Sipho followed him out into the road, waiting for his coin. The door slammed shut in his face. Perhaps the man would roll down the window to pass him something. Instead the engine started up and, without even glancing at him, the man swung the truck out into the road. Sipho sprang back just in time. An elderly black man, walking slowly up the hill, stopped to lean on his stick. He must have seen Sipho leaping out of the way of the truck.

"Are you all right, my son?" he asked.

"*Yebo, baba.* Thank you."

Shaking a little, Sipho returned to the pavement. Pressing his lips together, his fists clenched, he sprinted down the hill.

Sipho sat down outside Checkers, leaning against the plate glass window. He rested his head on his knees. Inside he was feeling small and angry. Like when his stepfather beat him and he was powerless against someone so big.

"*Heyta*, new boy! Are you hungry?"

In an instant, Sipho's eyes traveled from a battered pair of Doc Martens on the pavement up to the face with a scarred cheek. The figure blotted out the sun, casting a shadow over him. His churned-up feelings kept him tongue-tied. When his lips parted, no sound came out.

"Let me see your money. I'll go inside and buy you something. I like to help someone who's new."

Vusi's voice was soft but insistent, and he was holding out his hand. Sipho glanced rapidly around to see if Jabu or Joseph was in sight. But there was no one else he recognized. Not even Lucas. He didn't want to get on the wrong side of Vusi. Slowly he put his hand into his right-hand pocket, pulled out the apple and then a fistful of coins. He tried not to take them all out, but he didn't want Vusi to see him fiddling inside the pocket or he might suspect there was more. Carefully he counted the coins under Vusi's watchful eye.

"One seventy, one eighty, one eighty-five, one ninety . . ." Only one fifty-cent piece was in his hand, which meant the other was still in his pocket.

"*Hawu!* You work like a slave for so little!" exclaimed Vusi. "Is that all they gave you?"

If he said yes, what if Vusi then made him pull out his pocket and found out he was holding something back? It would be best just to show everything now. Putting his hand back in, he brought out the remaining fifty-cent coin and three small single cents.

"*Ja!* Now we can get something better," said Vusi holding out his hand for the money. "Wait here till I come."

Sipho was still waiting when Jabu arrived and slid down beside him. He must have sensed something.

"Is something wrong?" he asked. Sipho told him first about the man in khaki.

"When that kind of person sits with a baboon you don't know which is the father and which is the son," Jabu commented dryly.

But when Sipho told him about Vusi, he hesitated before speaking. "You must be very careful with that one. He has a knife. But it's okay when Lucas is there."

Sipho swallowed and felt his mouth go dry at the thought of the knife. Jabu pulled out a carton of milk from the pocket in his jacket. He drank out of it, then passed it to Sipho. Offering Jabu the apple that Vusi had ignored, Sipho pulled out the second apple for himself. He had lost the money from his morning's work, but at least he was still all right.

Together they sat eating and watching the passersby. The boys who had been begging outside the bakery were no longer there, and a group of *malunde* were now standing and chatting by the corner. Suddenly they broke apart, some climbing on the backs of others.

Piggyback fight! There was no sign, however, of Vusi or Lucas. Nor could Sipho see Joseph.

"Where's Joseph?" he asked.

Jabu shrugged. "He's like a new baby. Anyplace he lies down, he sleeps."

Or he might have gone off to Rosebank, which, Jabu explained, was a good place to "ask money" because there were very rich people there.

The passersby were now walking around the piggyback fighters. Some looked cross, while others hardly seemed to notice them. Jabu jumped up.

"Hey, Sipho, get on my back!"

Sipho clambered up and in seconds was being propelled across the pavement into the middle of the gang of laughing, shouting and tumbling *malunde*. But the game stopped as suddenly as it had begun. A woman came out of Checkers warning that she would call the police if they continued to disturb the customers. Someone must have complained. Sipho slipped off Jabu's back, and together all of them hurried away. No one stopped to argue.

Police meant trouble. Not only could Sipho be sent back home, but he might get a terrible thrashing. Once, his stepfather had taken him to the police station and asked the policeman on duty to "teach him a lesson." It had started with a letter from school complaining that he wasn't doing his homework. The policeman hadn't asked Sipho for his side of the story. Like his stepfather, he didn't want to hear that the homework was difficult and how the teacher shouted that he was stupid if he said he didn't understand. How *could* he do his homework? When Ma had tried to stop his stepfather from taking him to the police, he had pushed her aside.

Just thinking about the police made the thumping start up inside him again, but it began to relax as he listened to the other *malunde*. Now that Checkers was well behind them, they were laughing. One of them pretended to be the manager, pointing and shaking a finger at them. They started joking about who had been the first to run away.

"*Ja!* Thabo ran like it was a spook chasing him!" jeered a boy wearing oversized trousers rolled up at the bottom of each leg.

"You lie! I'll spook you, Matthew!" retorted another.

The two boys started chasing each other, dashing in between the pavement stalls and parked cars until a man selling leather bags called out that he would catch them and deal with them if they didn't clear off. Were they really not scared of the police, Sipho wondered? Or were they just pretending, like he did sometimes too?

When the laughter died down, one of the boys turned to Sipho and asked who he was. This time Sipho didn't wait for each question but told them his name, where he had come from and how he had left home because of his stepfather. What he said was simply accepted, and the conversation drifted to which games shop they should visit. Passing a garbage can, the two boys who had been chasing each other stopped to look inside it. After a small, friendly scuffle, one came back with an empty plastic bottle.

Following the others through a doorway, Sipho entered a shop packed with people, brightly colored video screens and what sounded like a hundred different noises. Cars were screeching at high speed, bombs were dropping from planes, little figures were bouncing up and down steps, fists were smashing into faces, and the pictures were flickering and changing. Men, boys and a few girls were crowding around the machines. Jabu signaled to Sipho to come back outside. The two boys who had scuffled over the garbage can followed.

"Let's go the Amusement Center. It's not so busy there. Those guys are fixed to the machines," said Jabu, putting on the expression of someone hypnotized.

They all laughed. Sipho liked the way Jabu moved the eyebrows above his large eyes. His face seemed to tell a story by itself. Jabu introduced Sipho to the other two, Thabo and Matthew, and together they set off.

It wasn't far to the Amusement Center, which turned out to be the games shop where Sipho had stopped earlier that morning. The man with the black mustache was still there, standing at the entrance to the next shop, keeping an eye on his goods on the tables outside. Sipho was very surprised when the man recognized him.

"Back again!" he said, smiling.

"Yes, sir," said Sipho, not knowing how to respond. Quickly he followed the others into the shop.

"Does *umlungu* know you?" asked Jabu.

"No," replied Sipho, frowning. "He saw me this morning. It was the first time."

The friendliness was a little strange.

Inside, Sipho forgot everything except the excitement of trying to ride a high-speed motorbike without crashing and to fly a plane without being hit by an unknown enemy. Before he knew it, his money had run out. He had used the one rand taken from Ma's purse. It was lucky that Vusi hadn't made him empty both pockets. But now he had nothing. With the others still absorbed in their screens, Sipho joined the onlookers. Wincing as the motorbike rider diced with death, he pushed aside any pangs of hunger.

It was only as they left the games shop and set off once again down the street that he really came back down to earth. Instead of the man with the mustache, a woman in a black beret and a green smock stood outside the shop next door. Ma wore a smock just like that . . . and before he could blot it out, a picture of her came into his mind. She had probably been crying all day. Perhaps she had been searching for him. He could imagine her trying to walk quickly, holding her stomach. Feeling a sudden wetness in his eyes, he quickly blinked. No, he wasn't going to let himself think about Ma. She had married someone who hated him, Sipho, her own son. He had run away because of "him," but it was her fault too. He had to think about himself now, not her. And he didn't even know yet where he was going to sleep.

5. Drifting

✖✖✖✖✖✖

The rest of the afternoon was spent crisscrossing Hillbrow with Jabu, Matthew, and Thabo, going nowhere in particular. The others let Sipho wander along the pavement market stalls without rushing him. He was curious about everything. Leather bags, purses, cassette tapes, shampoo, combs, cigarettes, matches, colored groundnuts, wooden carvings, necklaces and bracelets made of beads . . . all of these things were spread out neatly on tables or blankets. Worried about being chased away, Sipho was careful not to go too close. Instead he watched customers pick up items and examine them before buying or bargaining with the trader. Sometimes the four of them shared a joke at what they saw.

They had stopped to follow some bargaining between a trader and customer when Sipho's eyes were drawn to a nearby table full of carvings. He had to stop himself from putting out his hand. Among the masks and heads carved in wood and stone stood a line of small wooden animals. Because they were small, he needed to peer closely at them. An almost black rhino with two horns, one big and one small, seemed to be running. One back leg was raised off the table. As Sipho crouched down to see it better, the creature seemed to stare at him from the black dot in the middle of its tiny white eye. He thought it appeared a little worried. Behind it was a fat elephant with its trunk in the air that made him want to laugh.

The color of the wood had given it brown stripes! If only he could pick them up and feel them. Like he did with the clay animals he used to make from red earth on the farm. Would the rhino stare at him from his other eye too? And would that eye be scared or fierce?

"You want to buy one? I'll give you a good deal. Only ten rand."

The trader's voice startled him, and he looked up into the face of a man whose skin appeared as deeply polished as the wood of the rhino.

"I like the rhino, *baba*, but I don't have money."

"Maybe you will earn it and come back one day, young man."

"*Yebo, baba*. I will try."

Casting a last glance at the animals, Sipho forced himself to leave and go back to the others.

Farther down the road at a shoe repair shop, Matthew handed Thabo the empty plastic bottle from his pocket, counted out five rand and went inside. When he came back he was carrying a small can. Moving into a narrow alley nearby, Matthew carefully poured the white liquid from the can into the bottle. Sipho knew it was glue. A boy at school had been expelled for selling it.

When Matthew and Thabo said they wanted to sit down for a while, Sipho asked Jabu if he could "park cars" with him. The pangs of hunger were now gripping him more tightly. They were lucky and after about half an hour had earned enough money to buy chips from a fast-food shop. Still eating, they joined a crowd surrounding two men playing *umrabaraba* with counters on the pavement. Matthew and Thabo were there too. Matthew was giggling, but Thabo was silent. It was a noisy game, full of drama. One player was accused of cheating because an onlooker had given him advice. Soon all the adults seemed to have taken sides. Worried that a fight might break out, the four boys slipped away from the center. A minute later, however, the argument was over and the boys wandered off.

Later in the afternoon they made their way down a hill to a busy junction, along which people traveled home from the city. At first

Sipho stayed on the side, watching the other three as they walked in between the rows of cars at the traffic lights, asking for money. The lines were long, and they had to dart out of the way just before the lights turned green.

Plucking up courage, he went farther down the road, and when the cars began to slow down he slipped in between them. A lot of the drivers kept looking ahead as if he wasn't even there. Their windows were tightly shut, but every now and again someone would roll down the window and drop a coin into his hands. In some cars there were children who stared at him from the backseats. However, when two children in school uniform—a girl and a boy— stuck out their tongues, Sipho made a face back. At first they looked surprised and he saw them say something to their mother. As she turned to glare at Sipho, the car behind her hooted. Her face twitched suddenly. The lights had turned green, and Sipho had to dash to the side!

The sun was going down, leaving deep red and purple stripes in the sky above the buildings on top of the hill. All the buildings had turned a shadowy gray. A light wind was beginning to blow, and Sipho felt the chill go right through him. Once again, he wished he had remembered to bring a second sweater with him before leaving home. Taking out the wooly cap he had stuffed into his pocket earlier in the day, he pulled it down over his head and ears. Jogging up and down also helped, especially when the lights were green and he had to stand aside as the cars swept by.

He was beginning to wonder when the others would want to move on, when he heard a high-pitched whistle from behind him. He swung around to see Jabu, Thabo, and Matthew already on the road back up to Hillbrow. Jabu was signaling to him. When Sipho joined them, they were exchanging news on their earnings. No one had earned more than a couple of rand. Thabo had been given a package of potato chips, and he shared them as they walked. Sipho told them about how he had made a face back at the rude schoolchildren.

"The schoolkids in the bus sometimes throw rubbish down on us!" Matthew told Sipho.

"Just let them show off their turkey tails on the street. Then you'll hear them shriek when we pull out their feathers!" boasted Thabo.

They walked quickly uphill. Jabu said that people in the bakery would be clearing up and they could buy any leftover bread cheaply. They arrived just in time. The front of the shop was closed, but the back door was still open, and they went inside. The manager seemed annoyed when he saw them.

"Do you think I want to stay here all night?" he complained.

But he took the money they offered and came back with two packages of rolls and a small loaf of bread.

"This is all that's left. You'll have to share. Now move on!"

Outside the bakery, Sipho listened as the others discussed whether to go directly back to the *pozzie*—their sleeping place. If Lucas was there, he might have made a fire, and at least they would be warmer there. Sipho was glad when they agreed to go. Already he was very tired. He hoped that when it was time to sleep he would be too tired to feel the cold.

Starting to walk downhill again, Jabu explained to Sipho that their gang had recently stopped sleeping in Hillbrow.

"The police chase us too much here," he told Sipho.

"And if the shopkeeper finds you in the morning by his door, sometimes he'll beat you . . . *shuup, shuup, shuup!*" added Matthew, whipping his arm up and down.

Two weeks ago, however, Lucas had found a small unused plot of ground near the railway line at Doornfontein where they could sleep. The only problem was that hoboes sometimes came to the plot to drink. The drinking often led to fighting, and the boys were worried the police would then come and take them all away. But at least Lucas had claimed one side of the plot for the *malunde*, and the hoboes stayed on the other side. Sipho thought of the man who had sworn at him that morning and hoped he wouldn't be there.

The streets were now brightly lit up. Even high above, the darkness of the night was broken by lights in the buildings towering upward. If he had been going back home through the shacks in the township at this time, everything would have been completely dark. When there was no moon, you had to fumble your way as best you could between the shacks. Here there were even shops still open, with lots of people walking around. Music drifted out from some of the cafes and bars. In the roads cars were pulling up or moving out, just as busy as during the day. However, the farther they walked down the hill, the quieter and darker it became.

At the bottom, they turned left. They were beginning to leave the very tall buildings behind. The wind rustled the leaves in the trees above them, and shadows seemed to dance around them as they moved from one pool of lamplight to the next. Jabu told Sipho that behind them was a park which was very dangerous, even in daytime. *Tsotsis* hung around there, and sometimes they would take one of the *malunde* if they wanted him for a robbery or some other bad thing.

"Okay, we also steal sometimes if we're hungry or need something," said Jabu, "but those *tsotsis*, they actually *like* killing!"

"*Ja*, and they like telling everyone how they cut up this one and stabbed that one," added Matthew.

As they turned into a narrower road without any traffic, Sipho could hear the sound of their footsteps. The others were now talking about a man called Peter who liked to finger his knife while forcing *malunde* to buy glue from him. A couple of times Sipho turned around to make sure no one was following them.

6. Under the Night Sky

Approaching the *pozzie*, they heard voices and the crackle of fire on the other side of the fence. Sipho was the last to squeeze between the broken planks. In the flickering light from the dancing flames, he immediately recognized the gang's leader, Lucas. Vusi was there too, standing close to the fire with a prong in his hand. The smell of sausages made Sipho feel terribly hungry.

"*Heyta, magents!* So, gentlemen, my sausages called your stomachs!"

Vusi's voice sounded quite friendly. Lucas greeted them as well. He made no comment on Sipho being there. It seemed he was accepted. Another boy was sitting on the ground near the fire. Crouching down near him and stretching his hands out toward the warmth, Sipho recognized Joseph in his army jacket. Joseph lifted one hand and waved it toward him.

"So you came with Jabu! That's good," he said. His voice was slightly hoarse and slurred. In his other hand he was holding something, which he brought up to his face. He took in a couple of sharp breaths. Then unexpectedly Joseph pushed the plastic bottle toward Sipho.

"Here," he said. "Take some. You'll feel nice. With *iglue* you won't be cold, you won't be hungry."

Sipho put out his hand to refuse. "I don't like it," he said quickly.

It was a lie. He had never tried it. When the glue pusher had been expelled from his school, his mother had made him promise her he would never use the stuff. By some good luck his stepfather didn't hear about the incident. *He* would probably have beaten Sipho just as a warning. That would have made Sipho so angry that he might have gone deliberately to look for some. But as it was, he hadn't gone around with a crowd that "smoked."

Joseph withdrew the bottle. A thin, wet trickle running down from his nose glinted in the firelight, until he roughly swept his sleeve across his mouth. After inhaling from the bottle again, he looked at Sipho through half-open eyes.

"It's okay," he said, pausing to cough as if trying to clear his throat. "But me, I'm having a good time. I have a nice, nice garden with lots of flowers. It's sunny . . . and hot . . . and I can sleep the whole day."

Tumbling over sideways, Joseph curled himself up and in an instant seemed to have fallen asleep. Sipho looked into the shadows, examining Joseph's "garden." The ground was rough and covered with tall grass except where it had been cleared. The fireplace was in the middle of the clearing. It was made of bricks covered with a metal grid, on top of which the sausages were now sizzling. A little distance away was a tree. It was difficult to see in the dark beyond the tree, but Sipho imagined that must be the part that the hoboes used when they came.

"Hey, new boy! Are you going to buy sausage from me? Only two rand each."

Vusi called out to Sipho from across the fire. He was holding up a sausage on the end of a knife. Vusi had taken more than two rand from him at Checkers. If only Sipho dared tell him "You owe me that!" Instead he pulled out the change he had left in his pocket. He was not used to money coming in and out of his pockets like this. That morning he had started off in Hillbrow with less than two rand and here he was, after a day of earning and spending, with just over two rand left. Enough for the sausage! Tomorrow he would have to earn what he needed for tomorrow.

Biting off a small piece of meat to eat with each chunk of bread, Sipho savored the flavor while listening to the news pass among the gang. Lucas and Vusi had gone to Rosebank. Lucas had wanted to buy new shoes, and by midafternoon they had each earned over thirty rand pushing carts, parking and washing cars. It must be some kind of fantastic place, thought Sipho, where people had so much money to pay *malunde*. Perhaps Jabu would take him there. He might even be able to earn enough to buy the little rhino!

"Do *malunde* sleep there?" he asked aloud.

Lucas shook his head. "The police swat us like flies in that place. They say they are keeping it clean."

After eating, most of the boys lit up *stompies* except for Jabu, who pulled out a full-length cigarette. Grinning, he boasted how he had slipped it off a table at the back of the bakery. The manager must have been about to smoke it when they arrived.

"He'll catch you next time!" said Thabo.

"*Hayi!* No!" laughed Jabu.

The manager had been so busy that he probably wouldn't be sure where he had left the cigarette.

With the fire dying down, Sipho felt the cold night air seeping in. However tightly he folded his arms and squeezed his legs together, the cold sneaked into him. When Jabu passed him his cigarette, Sipho took a puff and for a couple of seconds enjoyed the warm smoke swirling around inside his head. He was pleased with himself that he didn't cough. Shutting his eyes for a moment, he felt how heavy they were, but could he sleep when he was so cold? And if he was feeling this cold now, how did *malunde* manage right in the middle of winter?

"Lucas! The blankets are gone!"

Jabu's voice came urgently from a corner of the plot dimly lit by the dying fire. He had lifted up the cardboard they used for bedding to get the two blankets they had hidden that morning. Lucas began the questions. No one had been back to the *pozzie* during the day. Vusi shook Joseph, but he was still too dazed to make any sense. It was unlikely that he knew anything. It was far more likely that one of the hoboes had taken them and that was why they were not around tonight. When the thief came back, the blankets would already have been traded and no one would be able to prove anything.

As the gang settled themselves down together on the cardboard, Sipho listened to other tales of theft.

"I was fast asleep and they cut my pocket! And that time I had ten rand!" Matthew complained.

"*Ja,* when you sleep, you don't know anything,"

said Thabo. "One time I was feeling cold so I woke up. But it was too late. My blanket was already gone!"

"You have to sleep on top of your blanket. Then it's safe," added Jabu.

Was Jabu serious or joking, Sipho wondered? It was harder, however, for him to know whether to believe Vusi's story. It was about how an old lady he always helped at Checkers had given him a blanket at Christmas. Sipho just couldn't imagine Vusi helping an old lady.

"But then the policeman came and made me give him the blanket," continued Vusi. "When I asked him why, he said I must be a thief to have such a nice new blanket!"

Everyone agreed that as *malunde*, anything bad could happen to you and there was nothing you could do.

Sipho lay near the edge of the cardboard, his head resting on Jabu's shoulder and his body curled up against him. Except for Joseph, who was still lying fast asleep by himself, the gang lay closely against each other. Sipho had placed himself, though, on the opposite side of the heap from Vusi. It made him uneasy to think of someone with a knife lying so close to him. Before long the chatting had stopped. Listening to the sounds of breathing, Sipho wondered if he was the only one still awake. The cold clutched at his toes and back, wherever it could get hold of him. Was it possible that Joseph really didn't feel the cold because of *iglue*? Was that why Matthew and Thabo had been sniffing it too? Matthew lay close to him now. If he stretched out his hand he could touch him and find out if he was still awake. He could ask to try just one sniff to see if it worked . . . But what would Ma say if she knew?

Lying among the small heap of *malunde*, on a plot of open ground, with nothing between himself and the wide, black night sky, Sipho was suddenly overcome with the thought that Ma *wouldn't* know. He wasn't going to see her again. He had run away. He had no family anymore. The tears began trickling down his face before he could stop them. Wiping them away with his sleeve, he held his breath tightly to stop any sobs. He didn't want anyone to see or hear.

But someone did know. Someone was shuffling up to him and then pushing something into his hands in the darkness. Sipho jerked himself up, and Jabu groaned softly in his sleep.

"Quiet, man! It's only me! My nice dream went bad. A car came to knock me, then a snake came to eat me, and when I ran, I was swallowed by a big hole," whispered a husky voice.

It was Joseph. The thing being pushed into

Sipho's hands was the bottle of *iglue*.

"The first night is always bad. Me, I was only eight and I was crying all night because my ma, she didn't want me anymore. She said the social worker must take me away. But I ran far so they couldn't find me. Then a boy at Park Station gave me *iglue* to help me sleep."

Joseph settled himself down next to Sipho. Without stopping to think anymore, Sipho put the bottle up to his nose and took a couple of sharp, deep breaths.

"Take some more, man!" whispered Joseph.

Sipho sniffed again, until suddenly his head felt quite light, almost dizzy. He didn't like the feeling but lay down, resting his head again on Jabu's shoulder. With Joseph now on the other side of him, he felt warmer. It was good being close to somebody else. Joseph's mother hadn't wanted her son, and his own ma didn't care about him anymore. But now he was remembering how good it used to feel when as a very small boy he had slept alongside his grandmother. Her bed had always been so warm. Well, now he was a little boy once again with someone taking care of him, and he and Gogo were together in a warm place, floating, floating . . .

7. A Test for Sipho

✕◇✕◇✕◇✕

Sipho woke up with someone shaking him. For a few seconds he was startled, not knowing where he was. He was not on his mattress between the packing-box table and the stove. Instead of the dimness of the shack, light was attacking his eyes. Instead of his mother urging him to get up, in a soft voice that would not disturb his stepfather, it was Lucas silently shaking the boys who were still sleeping.

Although the sun was up, the hard earth was still cold beneath the thin cardboard, and Sipho's whole body was stiff. No one spoke much as they prepared themselves for the new day, slowly stretching their limbs and crossing to another corner of the plot where a small bush served as a toilet. Boys sat smoking their *stompies*, waiting for the sun to sink into them. Sipho rested his elbows on his knees and his head on his hands. The night before his head had felt so light; now it felt terribly heavy. Was it the effects of *iglue*? Surely not. He had only had a little. He must be getting a cold. If he had been at home Ma would have taken a few drops of oil from her special little bottle and rubbed it on his chest and back to help him breathe. He closed his eyes, trying to shut out the picture. He was aware that Joseph was half sitting, half lying, also holding his head in one of his hands. Was he feeling bad too, or was he just trying to remember his dream garden?

Sipho wasn't aware of any signal but, without anyone saying a word, the gang got up as if part of a single body, even Joseph. Jabu and Matthew stacked the cardboard in the corner of the plot before following the others toward the gap in the fence. Once out on the pavement they walked in the opposite direction from the one in which Sipho recalled coming the night before. A few cars were parked in the road, but apart from a man carrying a package and a couple of figures walking ahead of them in the distance, the street was still quiet.

The boys' silence was only broken when they reached a wire fence alongside a railway siding. No railway workers were in sight.

"It's fine," said Lucas. "Let's move!"

Slipping through a hole between the fence and the ground, the boys made their way to a tap at the back of an old brick building. Removing a loose brick, Vusi produced a piece of soap. It was passed to each one in turn as they ducked their heads under the water.

That seemed to bring people alive. When it was Jabu's turn, he came out from under the tap shaking the water off his head and sending a flicker down his body. Sipho was reminded of the puppy Gogo had got him. Once, when he was meant to be watering the garden, the farmer's son, Kobus, had got him to turn the hose on the puppy. They had laughed at the puppy's surprise and how it shook itself afterward. But ducking under the tap himself and feeling the icy cold shower hit his head brought Sipho firmly back to where he was . . . and his own head, which was still hurting.

More awake now, the gang began chatting on their journey up to Hillbrow. By the time they had reached the top of the hill, they had split into twos and threes. Sipho walked with Jabu and Joseph, stopping with them to exchange greetings of "*Heyta, magents!*" and "How's your *scheme?*" with *malunde* who had spent the night in Hillbrow itself. Most of the talk was about a high-speed car chase in the middle of the night, but the cars had roared away and no one knew what had actually happened.

The rest of the day, and those that followed, took on a similar shape to Sipho's first day with the other *malunde*. They got money "parking" or washing cars, pushing *amatrolley* or "asking money" from motorists and customers from the restaurants, movie theaters, shops, and clubs. Sometimes they did odd jobs for shopkeepers, although there were some whom it was wiser to avoid. Sipho heard about sleeping children having cold water thrown over them or being beaten when found in a shop entrance. But the man with the droopy black mustache, selling jeans and T-shirts at Danny's Den next to the video games shop, didn't fit that picture. When he saw Sipho he greeted him and after a couple of days asked if Sipho would sweep his floor, giving him one rand. The next day Sipho was asked to help unload and unpack a delivery of shirts.

"You're quite a smart boy, you know," the man said to him, paying him two rand this time.

Sipho smiled, both at the coins and at the compliment. Mr. Danny Lewis, of Danny's Den, puzzled him.

In between the business of getting money and food, there were various ways to pass the day . . . riding carts . . . mock fighting . . . or, if they had small change to spare, playing video games and gambling on *tiekie-dice*. At other times, they just sat watching the rest of the world go by. Each day was different, yet the same. To eat, you had first to get money. And every night the same bitter wind gripped Sipho's bones, stopping his cold from getting better.

On his second day Joseph told him where he could buy some *iglue* for himself. For a couple of days he resisted, remembering the terrible way his head had ached. He wasn't sure whether it had come from his cold or from *iglue*. But when he couldn't get to sleep at night and lay awake shivering, he was tempted. He tried to imagine he was floating away in a warm bed, but it was no good. On the fourth night, the wind was even sharper, making the fire struggle to keep alight. Sipho tapped Joseph urgently on the arm as they huddled down on the cardboard preparing to sleep.

"Please, give me *iglue*. I'll get more for you tomorrow," he promised.

In his pocket he had a few small coins he had begun to save for the little wooden rhino. He would use those and the money he got at Checkers in the morning.

This time he didn't even stop to think of Ma's words before bringing Joseph's bottle up to his nose. His eyelids closed, and everything around him in the *pozzie*—including the other boys and the biting night wind—began to fade away as he sniffed in the fumes. But now something else seemed to be staring down at him. It was up there in the sky, getting bigger while he seemed to be getting smaller. The thing was white, with a black dot in the middle. It was an eye. Slowly a shape grew around it. When he saw the two horns and small ears, he knew what it was. The head of the little rhino. Except that it didn't seem so little anymore, looming high above him as he felt himself shrinking smaller and smaller. But its one eye still looked so very sad, as if it was lost. Sipho drifted into an uneasy, restless sleep.

It was Jabu who stopped him from going into the shoe repair shop the next morning.

"My friend died from this stuff," Jabu told him sharply. "We found the bag on his head. We took him to the hospital but he was already finished."

Overhearing Jabu's story, Joseph dismissed it roughly. "Your friend was stupid. You must use a bottle, not a bag."

Sipho saw the anger flash across Jabu's eyes. For a moment it seemed as if he might hit out at Joseph. But he lashed out with words instead.

"*Hayi, Bra* Joseph! It's you that's stupid! *Iglue* is making you sick and you can't even see. Did you forget about Jeff?"

Joseph sucked in his cheeks as if he was thinking of what to say. Then, folding his arms, he shifted his gaze upward, as if into space. He remained silent as Jabu told Sipho about a boy from another gang who had died with his head in a garbage can while looking for something to cool his throat. Word had gone round afterward that Jeff had pneumonia because his lungs were damaged from *iglue*.

Jabu spoke so forcefully that it took Sipho by surprise. "If you owe him, give him money, Sipho. Don't buy *iglue* yourself. It's no good!"

"But it helps me sleep when I'm cold. It makes me think I'm in some nice warm place," said Sipho.

"You need a jacket, not *iglue*, *buti*. I can take you to Rosebank and you can get enough money to buy one, even today."

Sipho hesitated. Jabu's offer was kind, and it made him think. While most members of the gang were taking the stuff—and Joseph more than any of them—he hadn't seen either Lucas or Jabu with *iglue*. It was one thing to sniff a little of your friend's supply and quite another to go and buy it yourself. But here was Joseph, who had been friendly to him, waiting now for him to do just that and return his favors. Joseph's face had no expression as he leaned against the shop front, but Sipho knew he was listening.

"Give him his money and let's go," said Jabu.

It was a test, and Sipho was right in the middle of it. He hated tests. He never knew the right answer. Putting his hand in his pocket, he pulled out all his coins.

"Take this, *buti*. I want to check out Rosebank. Will you come?" he said to Joseph.

Joseph leaned his head back and looked at him coolly. Then he shrugged and put out his hand for the money before turning his back and entering the shop.

8. Rosebank

Rosebank and the suburbs leading to it were another world. Jabu and Sipho walked past houses so large and grand that it was hard to believe that only one family lived in them all by themselves. Surrounded by high walls, most of them could only be glimpsed where there were metal or wrought-iron gates. Twenty or thirty shacks from the township would have fitted into some of the front gardens alone.

"See that wedding cake!" Jabu pointed to a house with pillars in front of a great door and triangle shapes above all the windows. The windows themselves were covered by curling burglar bars. Water was sprinkling gently in circles on a green lawn almost as smooth as a carpet.

"Look how much water these people give to their grass!" exclaimed Sipho.

One of the jobs he used to do for Ma was to line up with the crowds at the tap and carry a large plastic container of water back to the shack. Would Ma now be doing that herself?

"My aunty worked in a big house like this in Durban," said Jabu.

"Were you in Durban?" Sipho was impressed.

Gogo had told him about the city by the sea, which she had visited as a girl.

Jabu explained that he had lived with his mother in the hills behind Durban and sometimes they had visited his mother's sister in the city. But then the killings had started. And the burning. One night they had fled into the bushes and watched flames eat up the houses of their neighbors on the other side of the valley. Those people liked Mandela, said his mother. They wanted him to be the president and carried his picture at their meetings. That was why some men set their houses on fire. He had heard terrible cries, and he didn't know if they came from people or animals. The smell carried by the wind had made him sick. What had happened to the children from those houses who went to his school? In the morning the green hill opposite was scarred with black patches and burned-out buildings. His mother had decided to send him to her brother in Jo'burg for safety. But his uncle's wife didn't want him and so he had run away to get away from her beatings.

The two boys kept on walking all the while Jabu spoke. Sipho listened closely. He admired Jabu for being able to talk so calmly about these things. If only he could tell Jabu his story too . . . why he had run away. But it still upset him too much. Seeing the water sprinkling the grass and the brief thought of Ma, with her big stomach, carrying a heavy container of water all the way from the tap had already disturbed him. He didn't want to cry, like he had done the other night.

By the time they reached Rosebank they were hot and thirsty. Compared with Hillbrow, the roads seemed wider and less crowded and the buildings, although big, not as high. A couple of women sat on a pavement selling bead necklaces and bracelets. Their goods were spread out on blankets in front of them, and one of them was arguing with a customer.

"No, madam, I can't sell it more cheap! To make that necklace, I must work many hours."

The seller shook her head. She was frowning underneath the black scarf tied around her head.

"I'll give you ten rand for it. I've seen the same necklace for ten rand in Durban."

The lady who was trying to bring down the price dangled the necklace of light and dark blue beads in her hand. The necklace and bracelet she was wearing herself glinted in the sun. Were they gold, thought Sipho? The same thought must have struck Jabu.

"That lady is rich but she doesn't like to

spend her money!" he whispered.

"*Ja*, I think she hides it under her mattress," giggled Sipho.

The seller kept shaking her head, saying something under her breath. It was in Zulu but not clear enough for Sipho and Jabu to hear.

"Well, how about twelve rand, then?" said the lady.

"All right, the madam can have it for twelve rand."

The lady's red lips stretched into a smile as she lifted a ten-rand note and a couple of coins from her handbag.

"Thank you," she said.

But the seller wasn't smiling as she took the note and folded it carefully into a small, worn purse.

Sipho followed as Jabu turned into a paved street where there were no cars but people were walking by, while others were browsing in shop windows or sitting at an open-air cafe. Behind the tables with umbrellas, tall jets of water were splashing from a fountain, which made Sipho's mouth feel even drier. Two guards in maroon uniforms, carrying mobile telephones, stood in the sun chatting to each other. They seemed too busy in conversation to notice the boys passing them.

Inside, the shopping center glittered with

lights even though it was the middle of the day. With great glass windows in the shops, as well as panels of polished brass and steel, the place seemed full of mirrors and reflections. Sipho remembered his surprise at some of the prices in the Hillbrow shops. But here the prices were even higher. Over R2,000 for a man's jacket and nearly R200 just for a tie! In one window, a carpet with pretty patterns had a label saying R8,695! Traveling up a moving staircase, Sipho looked down at people walking below and wondered how some people could get so much money. It was noticeable that, unlike in Hillbrow, most of the shoppers here were white. But when a smartly dressed black couple passed them, he watched curiously as they entered a shop selling men's clothes.

Following the sound of music, they found a white woman playing the piano at a cafe. Tables and chairs were spread "outdoors," although they were covered by the enormous roof of the shopping center. For a few moments they stood watching the pianist's fingers scuttling over the keys and listening to the tinkling melody. Sipho pursed his lips at the smell of coffee and freshly baked buns.

"*We bafana*! You boys! Clear off!"

A waiter was coming toward them, making sweeping movements with his arm.

"Sorry, *baba*, sorry. We only ate the food with our eyes and the music with our ears!" Jabu called behind him as they quickly moved off, not waiting for the reply.

The waiter might inform a guard, who would chase them away from the center. It was a strange place, Jabu explained to Sipho as he led him outside to the supermarket exit. Rosebank people had a lot more guards to chase you away, but they usually gave much bigger tips when they paid you!

What Jabu said was true. Within half an hour of helping shoppers, Sipho had already earned twice as much as he would have earned in Hillbrow. Here people often gave him fifty cents and sometimes even a whole rand at a time. Seeing him sweating, one shopper also gave him a can of Coke. Pushing *amatrolley* was easier here too because there was no hill to struggle up.

After a couple of hours, they decided to change their work and help motorists park. While some people shooed them away, most let them get on with their work and paid them. By the middle of the afternoon, Jabu said they should return to Hillbrow. It had been a good day and they had been lucky. They could even afford to treat themselves to a burger and chips and travel back by bus. Sipho had never had so much money of his own before. He could come back here another day to earn the money to buy the little rhino! With twenty-five rand in his pocket, he had to stop himself from taking it out to count and letting other people know he was rich! He had already heard plenty of tales about *malunde* being robbed, and he didn't want it to happen to him.

Back in Hillbrow, Jabu led the way to the secondhand store. Behind the furniture were clothes and in the corner was a rail of army jackets, like Joseph's. They cost twenty-four rand, and as soon as he had seen them, Sipho knew he wanted to try one on. Still he hesitated. Most people he knew distrusted the uniform and the soldiers who wore it. People kept saying that things were meant to be changing, but where was this thing called change?

"Come on, man, try it!" said Jabu, taking a jacket off the rail.

Sipho slipped his arms through the sleeves and did up the buttons. Then he looked at himself in the mirror of a nearby wardrobe. He was aware of the shop assistant's eyes on him. He straightened his back.

"You can be a soldier for Mandela when he is president!" said Jabu, grinning.

Sipho placed his money on the counter and

kept the jacket on even though the afternoon was still warm from the sun. It was only as they were walking down the street that it occurred to him that while the army jacket might keep Joseph warm, it still hadn't stopped him wanting *iglue.*

9. Night Attack

XOXOXOX

Something was wrong, and Sipho and Jabu knew it as soon as they entered the street leading to the *pozzie*. No orange sparks flickered in the dark above the fence. Instead of the muffled sounds of ordinary talk carried in the air, they were struck by the loud noise of an argument. One voice was that of Lucas, but the others were unfamiliar to Sipho, except that one of them carried an unpleasant ring. It was a deep, rough voice and almost every second word seemed to be "blerry."

Climbing through the fence, his eyes needed time to sort out the figures in the dark. Suddenly Sipho realized whose voice it was. The bushy-haired, red-faced man who had shouted at him on his first day in Hillbrow!

"*Hayi!* These people, they always make trouble for us!" Jabu said softly. He was sure they had stolen their blankets and then sold them. By now they would have already spent the money, most likely on drink. "They think they can do anything with *malunde*," he added.

The argument raged. It seemed that Lucas and the others had found the three hoboes settled on their side of the plot. They had taken the *malunde*'s cardboard to use themselves and were refusing to move. Lucas kept his voice steady as he repeated how they had agreed that the tree in the middle of the plot would mark their areas. Then Vusi cut in.

"First you steal our blankets, now you want to steal our place!" he said.

"You blerry brat! I'll fix you good and proper!"

The speaker tried to lunge forward but was held back by his friends. Lucas's hand shot out to restrain Vusi too. Even in the darkness, Sipho could see that none of the hoboes were very steady on their feet. He was a little surprised to realize that one of them was a woman. It was she who ended the argument, persuading the other two that they would have a better time "downtown." As the three of them finally shuffled out of the *pozzie*, the bushy red-face growled a warning that they had all "blerry better watch out."

Later, sitting around a small fire, the gang talked about different kinds of threats. Sometimes people carried them out but sometimes they didn't. They just wanted to frighten you.

"*Cha!* No one tries nonsense like that with me twice. I want to give that *Matomatoes* a lesson," declared Vusi.

Sipho had to smile at the name "Matomatoes." He wondered if Vusi really would have used his knife if Lucas hadn't stopped him.

"Sometimes it's better to let things cool," said Lucas firmly.

Everyone knew that Matomatoes always swore at *malunde*, and Lucas thought he wouldn't actually do anything. But Sipho still remembered his bloodshot eyes from that first day, and they disturbed him.

Joseph occasionally sniffed from his plastic bottle, and Sipho was glad that nothing was said about what had happened in the morning. As they lay down to sleep, Joseph even joked that Sipho had got a jacket like his own. But although the jacket helped, it still could not keep out the cold night wind that whipped around the *pozzie*. Nor could it keep out all those thoughts that came late at night to keep him awake . . . of Gogo telling him stories before he slept, of his puppy wagging its tail and asking to play, of Ma visiting them on the farm, in the time before "him" . . .

Sipho must have fallen asleep. Because the next thing he knew was that he was waking up in the terror that usually came from a nightmare. The kind of nightmare in which his stepfather turned into a monster with ten heads and ten pairs of arms and legs. In this terror now, however, there were screams and shouts and the sharp pain of a boot being kicked into his ribs. Thick hands were grabbing him. He tried to struggle, but he was caught in a vise, squeezing his wrists and twisting his arms behind his back. In the beam of a light flashing wildly, he saw the writhing bodies of the other boys and the grinning faces of their captors. They were being hauled across the *pozzie* out into the road and then thrown into the back of a *gumba-gumba*, a dreaded police van. Lucas, the last to be slung in, fell like a sack of potatoes, and the van doors were banged shut.

For a minute no one said anything. Sipho was shaking. Jabu was holding his side and whimpering. Everyone was in shock. Then the silence broke in the dark.

"What do they want with us?"

"Who are these people?"

"Police! Only police drive *gumba-gumbas*."

"But they don't have uniforms."

"They take off their uniform when they want to do something bad so you can't say for sure it's them."

"They stole my knife! If I had my knife I would kill them!"

Sipho clutched himself more tightly, his eyes adjusting slowly to the darkness. Lucas was painfully lifting himself up. He spoke quietly.

"We don't know how many of these are police. They can get into trouble for this kind of thing now."

Perhaps only one or two were actual policemen, continued Lucas. The others could be their friends . . . the kind of white people who didn't want any change in the country . . . who wanted to keep black people down forever and who didn't want them to vote in the elections for the new government.

Suddenly from outside the van there was a burst of laughter. A few seconds later the van doors were wrenched open. Sipho made out a hand being thrust in, then the sound of squirting. Even before the hand was pulled back and the door slammed shut, something was in their eyes, their nostrils, their mouths. There was no air left to breathe, only something horribly foul stifling them. It smelled like the spray for killing insects. Coughing and trying to cover his mouth at the same time, Sipho felt he was going to be sick.

Now the *gumba-gumba* was moving, its engine revving and rumbling. Where were they being taken? It felt like they were traveling fast, only occasionally slowing down. Together they clustered at the far end of the van, holding on to each other, holding their stomachs tightly or trying to bury their faces and stinging eyes in their arms.

Suddenly the van gave an enormous shudder, and Sipho found himself flung forward as it came to a bumping halt. He was the first to be grabbed as the door swung open.

"Okay, *vuilgoed*! Rubbish like you can get a nice wash here!"

Ahead of him, glinting through the darkness, Sipho saw water. He screamed as he was picked up. He tried to struggle once again, but it was no use. The hands and arms were too powerful for him as they threw him out into the lake.

Hitting, then breaking through the ice-cold water, his body shot out arms and legs in all directions. He couldn't swim. The more he fought with the water to get back up, the more he felt it pulling him down. He was spluttering. The water was in his nose, in his mouth . . . He couldn't breathe. He was sinking, his body pierced by a thousand freezing shocks.

Then a hand grasped his arm and he felt himself being slowly tugged until his foot touched something. Something solid that wasn't sinking beneath him. He brought his other foot down. He was standing! Stretching, he got his head enough above the water to gasp and gulp at the air. The hand led him on a few more paces and then let go. A figure dived away from him. He was too confused to know who it was. Cries mingled with wild splashing sounds. On the bank ahead, he could just make out two large figures throwing a struggling shape out into the lake. Lucas? Laughter floated over to him. The *gumba-gumba* was revving up again. Within seconds the men had all climbed inside and disappeared into the night.

Underneath his feet, Sipho felt things that were sharp. Painfully edging step by step, he forced himself forward through the water. His clothes, dripping and sticking to his body, felt unusually heavy. Shivering uncontrollably, he waded at last to the water's edge, pulled himself onto the bank and flung himself down on his back. Directly above, as if staring down at him from the ink-black sky, was the moon, pale and white. Like a face. Was it laughing too?

One by one the other *malunde* joined him, shaking, swearing, sobbing. Jabu was the last. His head bobbing in and out of the water, going down here and coming up there, he guided those who were struggling toward the bank. Such a strong swimmer . . . where did he learn it? thought Sipho. And weren't his feet stinging too? Sipho pulled off his soaking canvas shoes. The thin soles were torn, and his feet were cut and bleeding. It was the same with the others. People had thrown bottles into the lake, which were lying at the bottom, broken and sharp. Joseph and Matthew, however, emerged in an even worse state. Finding bottles of *iglue* in their pockets, their attackers had emptied them over their hair.

With water dripping from his clothes and trembling like the others, Lucas insisted they leave immediately before any police arrived, but this time in uniform.

"They can charge us with trespass!"

They could even be the same men who had thrown them into the lake, but who would ever believe *malunde*?

10. Shelter in a Doorway

No one was sure of the way, and the streets were confusing. Main roads had to be avoided wherever possible, just in case the *gumba-gumba* or a police car appeared. Passing by houses behind locked gates, they were alarmed when dogs sniffed them and began to bark. If someone saw them, they might think they were thieves and call the police. But when they came to a small shopping center and saw ahead of them a night watchman by a fire, they decided to take a chance. Lucas indicated that Sipho should come with him while the others remained behind in the shadows.

"*Sawubona, baba,* good evening. May we warm ourselves by your fire for a short while, please?" Lucas began.

"*Hawu, bafana!* Why are your clothes so wet, my children?" asked the watchman. He was an elderly man and wore a blanket over his shoulders.

"Some men caught us and threw us in the water, *baba*," Lucas replied.

"What kind of men can do that to children?" said the old man.

"We don't know who they are, only they were in a *gumba-gumba* and we did nothing to them," continued Lucas. "But *baba*, we have more friends who are also cold and wet. Can they come to the fire too, *baba*?"

The watchman studied their faces closely for a couple of seconds and then nodded. Sipho turned and called the others.

The watchman made tea for them as they huddled by his fire. Shaking his head at times, he listened to them as they talked while passing the hot mug from one to the other.

"Police! They should be helping to stop all this violence. How can we have peace when police also do these things?" he commented bitterly. He asked the question in a tone that didn't expect a reply. But then, looking directly at Lucas, he asked, "Are police always doing this to you?"

"Some of them give us a hard time, hitting and chasing us. But not all of them, *baba*."

Lucas told the story of a policeman who had arrested four white boys after they had been chasing *malunde* with bicycle chains. There were also some policemen who asked *malunde* to wash their vans, giving them bread and tea and even a bit of money. But mostly, police gave them trouble.

"Like that time they forced us to drink *mbamba*," added Jabu, screwing up his mouth. "Then they took us to the police station to punish us because we were drunk!"

Fixing his eyes on Jabu and Sipho next to him, the old man said, "My grandson, he is the same size like you. My heart would be very sore if he was on the streets like you children."

Before they left, the watchman pointed out the best route to Hillbrow. They thanked him for his kindness. Their clothes were still wet, but no longer dripping. Sipho felt that the worst of his trembling had passed. In Hillbrow they would try to sort themselves out. Lucas said they should also spend a few nights there, in case there was another attack on the *pozzie*. In the meantime he would look for another place for them.

The stars were fading and the sun just coming up by the time they were within reach of Hillbrow. It was best to split up in case the police were still patrolling. They could meet by Checkers later, when the streets were busier. Members of the gang branched off into different streets until only Sipho and Jabu were left. They were entering Hillbrow, with tall buildings on either side.

"See you later, *buti*!" Jabu said, as he too turned off into a side street.

Sipho continued up the hill. His torn canvas shoes padding on the pavement seemed to echo behind him. Lights in the windows high above showed that people were beginning to wake, but the street was still strangely quiet in the half-light. A man walking a dog on a leash tugged it away from Sipho as they passed. He would have liked to say hello to the little dog, which had tufts of long hair over its eyes, but the man didn't look very friendly. Each time a vehicle passed Sipho turned to be sure it was not the police, but most times it was just another early-morning taxi.

Perhaps it was the chance of warming himself inside the video games shop when it opened that led Sipho in the direction of the street where he had first arrived in Hillbrow. It seemed more than just a few days ago. The grille across the front meant he couldn't shelter there. But perhaps he could wait in the entrance to Danny's Den. He hoped Mr. Danny wouldn't mind. Feeling suddenly so tired that he could hardly think straight, he sank down outside the shop door. Clasping his arms around him, as if that could get rid of the horrible cold, sweaty damp, Sipho rolled over onto the pavement. It was hard and hurt his head. He no longer had his wooly cap. Had it been pulled off him or come off as he hit the water? He didn't know. Nothing mattered now except sleep.

"Hey, Dad! This kid's clothes look quite damp! He's shivering in his sleep!"

"Well, he can't sleep here. We have to open the shop in half an hour."

"He's only a kid, Dad! It's disgraceful any kid has to live like this!"

The sound of voices made Sipho jerk up. He didn't want any more kicks in the ribs.

"Oh, so it's you!" said the man's voice.

Sipho wiped his sleeve across his eyes and looked up at the mustached face of Mr. Danny.

"Sorry . . . sorry, sir. I'm just going," stammered Sipho, pushing himself up.

"Don't you know you get sick like that, sleeping in wet clothes!" said Mr. Danny.

"Hold on, Dad! He probably couldn't help it! How did you get so wet?" said the tall girl next to him.

She had long hair the color of ripe *mealies*, and her deep-blue eyes looked straight into Sipho's. He didn't know what to say. Would these people believe him?

"Was it a prank, hey? You and your friends messing around?" Mr. Danny ventured.

"No, sir! We weren't messing, sir! We weren't doing anything bad, sir! These men came while we were sleeping . . ." Before he had even time to think, Sipho blurted out the events of the night.

The grabbing, the kicking, the screaming, the shouting, the journey in the *gumba-gumba* . . . being flung into the lake, not being able to swim . . . walking back frozen, soaked and with cut feet . . .

As he told the story, Sipho didn't look at Mr. Danny and his daughter. In front of his eyes he saw all the awful things happening over again. He wrapped his arms tightly around himself, and when he finished speaking there was silence. Then he cast a quick glance at the girl's face. It was clouded, and her blue eyes were no longer so clear.

"I think you had better come inside," said Mr. Danny quietly. "We can find you something dry to put on."

At the back of the shop was a little office with a couple of chairs next to a cluttered desk. Mr. Danny's daughter pulled out a small electric fire from under the desk and turned it on.

"You can sit here," she said. "Dad's getting you some clothes. By the way, what's your name?"

"Sipho," he replied just as Mr. Danny came into the room.

"Here, try these, Sipho," he said, holding out a green sweatshirt and a pair of black jeans. He pointed to a couple of smocks hanging behind the door. "You can wear one of those on top. When you've warmed up, you can come and give me a hand in the shop if you feel up to it."

Mr. Danny turned to his daughter. "Come on, Jude. We'd better hurry up if we're to open on time. Maria should have been here by now. She was late last Saturday too. I'll have to dock her pay if this goes on. These people always have some excuse!"

"Maria is not 'these people,' Dad! She's herself!"

"I don't care who she is. I just want her to be on time!"

Sipho was left alone in the office. His fingers quivered and fumbled as he undid the buttons of his jacket. He sighed. It had looked so smart when he had put it on the day before. And how strange this was! Only on very special occasions had Ma ever been able to give him new clothes. Mostly he wore clothes passed on from one person to the next. Once stripped, he rubbed himself briskly all over with the flat palms of his hands, feeling also the rays of warmth coming from the red electric bar. He didn't want to cover up the new sweatshirt and jeans, but Mr. Danny had asked him to put on the smock. It was long for him, reaching almost to his ankles. What would Ma say if she could see him now in a smock like hers and if she knew what had happened to him? Turning his shoes upside down, he examined the holes before placing them close to the electric fire next to his damp bundle of clothes. He was wondering whether to crouch by the fire or sit on the chair when he heard the voices of Mr. Danny and his daughter coming from the shop. The girl's voice was high and clear.

"But, Dad, what are you going to do? Police are meant to help children, not harm them!"

Mr. Danny's voice was too low to hear properly, but Sipho made out something about a job.

"Dad, it's not just a job he needs. He needs somewhere to sleep! Somewhere safe."

Just then they were interrupted by someone, and Mr. Danny sounded angry. Moments later the office door swung open. A large woman walked in, frowning. Her wide brown forehead was glistening with sweat under a black beret. It was Maria. She had been friendly to him when he had done odd jobs for Mr. Danny in the front of the shop. When she saw him now, her frown changed to surprise. Reaching for the other green smock behind the door, she greeted Sipho and asked if something was wrong. Before he could say anything, Mr. Danny's daughter slipped in and took her hand.

"Come, Maria. If you make us all a cup of tea, Dad will calm down and I'll tell you everything."

11. Danny's Den

Slowly Sipho chewed the last corner of the thick slice of bread and jam that Maria brought him. He washed it down with a final mouthful of tea. What was it Mr. Danny had said? That he should come and help in the shop if he felt "up to it"? The terrible tiredness had gone, and he was feeling a lot better with his new dry clothes and some food in his stomach. But what about Jabu and the others? Had any of them had his luck? Had Joseph and Matthew found someone to help them get the *iglue* out of their hair? Perhaps he should go and look for them. Yet how could he help them?

At that moment Mr. Danny put his head around the door. "Ah, Sipho. That's good. You're looking a lot better. You can come and help me now."

Sipho followed him out through the shop to the entrance. Mr. Danny's daughter was taking money at the cash register and she smiled at Sipho as he went past.

"What I want you to do, Sipho"—Mr. Danny paused showing him two brightly colored T-shirts still in their plastic covering—"is to take these and stand by the corner. You show them to people and tell them 'Special offer! Fifteen rand! Only at Danny's Den!'"

"Yes, sir," replied Sipho.

Mr. Danny's mustache twitched with a sudden chuckle.

"Perhaps you'd look better without that big smock. Then people can see how nice the new sweatshirt looks on you too!"

"Yes, sir," replied Sipho, slipping off the smock and exchanging it for the T-shirt packages Mr. Danny held out for him.

Sipho placed himself at a spot where the sun shone on him. It was getting warmer, but it wasn't *that* warm yet. Holding up a green T-shirt in one hand and a red one in the other, he began to call out, "Special offer! . . ."

The sun had passed its high point when Mr. Danny's daughter came to ask if he wanted something to eat.

"Thank you, miss!" His voice was getting a little hoarse and he needed a break.

"My name is Judy," she said firmly.

What did she mean, thought Sipho? On the farm he had been taught to call white children "missie" or "baasie." Even his grandmother used to call them that. But calling Kobus, his playmate, "little master" stuck in his throat, and he had never called him that when they were on their own. It was stupid, but if you didn't say it the farmer and his wife would say you were getting cheeky. They might even tell your grandmother you must be taught a lesson.

"Dad says you'll make a good salesman," Mr. Danny's daughter continued as they walked back to the shop. "He reckons we've had more customers, even for a Saturday."

Judy—as she insisted Sipho should call her—shared her sandwiches and tried to make conversation as they sat in the office. He could see she was trying hard to be friendly. But he still felt awkward, and when she asked whether he had any parents, he shook his head.

"Oh, I'm so sorry," she said quietly.

Sipho kept his eyes down. The lie was out before he had even thought about it. But wasn't it safer that way? If these people knew he had a mother, he could be taken back to her, and then . . . Ma would be crying and he would be crying, clinging, clinging to her, until her husband would rip him away to give him "the lesson" he would never ever forget. It was too terrible to think about. Trying to wipe out the picture, Sipho looked to see what had happened to the pile of clothes he had left by the fire. Judy read what was now in his mind.

"Maria rinsed out your clothes. They're drying out in the back. You should have seen her face when she smelled them! That water must have been really bad where they threw you."

"*Ja*, it was," replied Sipho, pursing his lips.

He didn't want to seem rude, but he didn't know what to say to this girl.

From his position on the corner, where he spent most of the afternoon calling out about Danny's Den, Sipho kept a lookout for members of the gang. None of them came by. A couple of *malunde* whom he knew by sight passed him, and he asked if they had seen Lucas or any of the others. But they had been away in Rosebank all day and hadn't even heard of the raid.

Later in the afternoon, Mr. Danny called him inside to help sweep up in the shop. Maria had already brought in the tables from outside and tidied the shelves and was ready to leave as Sipho took up the broom. He would have liked to leave earlier too, so he could look for his gang. The thought of sleeping on his own frightened him more than ever now. But Mr. Danny hadn't given him a chance to say anything before giving him another job. He also needed to collect his own clothes. With the sun going down, it was becoming cold again and he wanted his sweater and jacket. Would Mr. Danny ask him to give back the sweatshirt and jeans, he wondered?

"Count this up, will you, Jude?" said Mr. Danny, carrying the small packages next to the cash register into the office.

He pulled the door behind him, but it remained slightly ajar. Alone in the shop, Sipho swung the broom into action, making little piles of dirt before sweeping them all together into the center of the room. The voices of Mr. Danny and his daughter were low, but as Sipho approached the office to collect the small dustpan behind the door, he heard his name and stopped.

"It's not quite so simple, Jude," Mr. Danny was saying. "I agree he seems a nice enough kid, but we don't really know him. It's one thing to give him some clothes and a bit of work. It's quite another thing to take him home with us."

"So you're happy to leave him sleeping out here when you know he could get beaten up again?"

"I'm not happy about it and you know it. But where do you stop, Jude? Hundreds . . . thousands of children don't have proper homes, safe homes. I can't solve all that!"

"We're only talking about Sipho, Dad. And he hasn't even got a home. He's an orphan!"

Sipho's brow furrowed as he tried to follow what they were saying. Did Judy want him to go home with them?

"And what about David? You know how difficult he's become since your mother left." Mr. Danny's voice was becoming less forceful.

"David'll be all right, Dad. You've just got to stop giving in to him all the time. He's really playing on your weak spots. It'll do him good to have to do a bit of sharing," Judy replied.

They continued to talk, and Sipho continued to listen. He still only understood bits of what they were saying. Who was this David? What was it Mr. Danny had said about the mother having left? What was so strange to him, however, was how Judy was talking to her father. She didn't seem at all scared to say what she wanted.

"Well, it can only be on a trial basis, do you understand, Jude?" Mr. Danny paused. "And I tell you, Jude, if Ada doesn't like him, he'll have to go. She's a good judge of people, and we'll know soon enough what she makes of this young man!"

"Okay! I agree!" Judy's voice rose. It sounded cheerful.

Sensing that Mr. Danny and his daughter were about to come out of the office, Sipho hastily knocked on the door.

"I need the dustpan, please," he said.

Mr. Danny looked at him steadily for a few moments, stroking down the ends of his mustache with his thumb and forefinger before running his hand back over his head as if to make his hair flat. Sipho watched the dark tufts bounce back up. Judy looked from her father to Sipho and back again.

"Look here, Sipho, I have a suggestion. I can give you somewhere to sleep at my house for the time being, and in the daytime you can come to work here in the shop. We can see how that works. What do you say?"

Sipho didn't know what to say. It was confusing. What would it be like to sleep in this white person's house? He had been waiting to finish his work so he could go and find Jabu and the others to see if they were all right. There was nowhere for them to sleep except on the streets. The pavements would be hard, freezing cold and also dangerous. And yet here he was being offered a place in a house, under a roof, and probably a bed with blankets.

"Why don't you just come with us and see." Judy offered, breaking the silence.

"Thank you, m . . ." He was about to say "miss," but stopped himself.

"Thank you, Mr. Danny, sir," he said.

12. A Warm Bed

>※<※<◎<※<※

From the back of Mr. Danny's car, Sipho thought he saw Jabu. But he couldn't be sure. They were driving past Checkers in the gray light that gets pulled over everything as the sun goes down. He had hoped the traffic lights would turn red to give him a chance to look properly. But they were green, and the car swept past the corner with only time for a quick glance at some figures crouched around a small fire on the other side of the road. One had a hood. That could have been Jabu.

Sipho recognized the place where he and the others "asked money" from motorists. A small boy, younger than him, was standing on the traffic island in the middle of the road as they drove past. Sipho could see him shivering a little. How odd it was to be in one of the cars, feeling warm air blowing from underneath the seat, and looking out at someone who was cold and alone.

Soon they had left the busy road with its moving streams of red and yellow lights and were traveling down streets with a mixture of houses and apartment buildings. Slowing down in front of a building with steps leading up from the pavement, Mr. Danny pressed his horn lightly. From behind the curtains of a second-floor window, Sipho saw a face appear and disappear.

"My friend Portia lives here," said Judy, turning around to Sipho. "She's coming over for the night."

"I can't understand how you girls find so much to talk about!" Mr. Danny joked. "I would have thought you saw enough of each other in school all week!"

"You're just antisocial, Dad!" retorted Judy, as a black girl in a pink track suit came running down the steps and waved up at the window above. Someone was holding a baby and waving the baby's hand. Judy leaned over to the back and opened the car door.

"Hi, Portia! Your little brother is so cute," she said, waving up at the baby.

Portia climbed into the backseat next to Sipho.

"Hello, Mr. Lewis! Thanks for collecting me," she said, smiling. "You know, Judy, my little brother isn't quite so cute when he cries at night!"

"Well, he's certainly cuter than my brother David!" replied Judy.

"That's hardly fair, Jude," reprimanded Mr. Danny.

Changing the conversation, Judy now introduced her friend to Sipho. The beads at the ends of Portia's braids clicked as she turned to greet him.

"Hi!" she said in a bright, chatty voice.

"Hi!" he replied softly.

Listening to the girls talking about homework, Sipho kept his gaze fixed outside. It was already quite dark, but these streets were well lit. Pulling up at some red lights, Mr. Danny pointed ahead of him. Scrawled on a white wall were the words VIVA MANDELA! VIVA ANC!

"They're not even in government yet, but see how they're already messing things up."

"Come off it, Dad! Nelson Mandela hardly went and wrote that himself! You're so prejudiced!"

Judy turned around to Portia in the backseat, making a face by casting her eyes upward. She looked embarrassed. Portia lifted her eyebrows but remained silent. There was something strange about Mr. Danny, thought Sipho. He could never imagine the white farmer sending his son, Kobus, to a school with black students. Or letting him bring home a black friend to sleep in his house. But Mr. Danny was doing that. So why didn't he like Nelson Mandela?

They had left all the apartments behind, and there were only houses on each side of the road now. Suddenly Mr. Danny swung the car in front of some iron gates. As if by magic, lights sprang up inside around a long, low house, partly hidden by bushes. Opening his window, Mr. Danny spoke into a small metal box on a pole and, as if by magic again, the gates slowly opened.

"I'm starving!" Judy declared as they drove in. "Ada doesn't know you're coming yet, Sipho, but she always makes more than enough. She knows Portia and I eat like horses!"

"Speak for yourself!" giggled Portia.

Before they had reached the front doorstep, Sipho heard chains jangling, barking, and the door being unlocked. A medium-sized dog with long, floppy ears bounded out, jumping, sniffing and licking.

"Get down, Copper!" ordered Judy.

Sipho put out his hand to stroke the dog, but, looking up at the woman who opened the door, he felt a sudden panic. She was small, like Ma, but looked older. Beneath her creased brown forehead, her eyes were like those of Gogo and the woman in the taxi. Deep, dark eyes that looked straight into you and knew if you were telling the truth. He had let these people think he was an orphan . . . Perhaps he should run right away. This whole place was strange to him. Lowering his eyes, he glanced quickly behind him—just in time to see the gate gliding back by itself, locking them in.

"This young man here is Sipho," Mr. Danny announced.

"Hello, Sipho. *Sawubona!*"

The voice of the woman at the door was firm. If she was surprised she did not show it.

"*Sawubona*, Mama!" he replied, keeping his eyes fixed on the pattern in the carpet as he stepped into the house. He was wearing his army jacket and the broken shoes, which were still damp, while carrying his other clothes bundled under his arm. Copper came leaping inside with them, trying now to sniff the clothes. The dog's long, wavy hair glowed with a reddish tint under the electric light.

"Copper, stop it! We're starving, Ada! Can we eat right away? We need to make one extra place."

Judy signaled to Sipho to follow her and Portia into a room with a long table covered with a white tablecloth. One end was set out with plates, knives and forks and shining glasses.

Apart from a narrow table at the side, there was no other furniture in the room, but on every wall there were pictures. Some large, some small, some with figures in them and some with just colors. There had been lots of pictures in Ma's shack too. She had papered the walls with pages cut from magazines. Lying on his mattress on the floor, he used to look up at film stars, or people smiling at him and telling him to buy something. These pictures were very different.

Sipho was still looking around when a boy entered the room who was about a head taller than him. In the car Judy had said her brother was three years younger than her, only eleven.

"This is my brother, David," said Judy.

The boy stared as Judy introduced him. His hair was darker than his sister's. It was like the brown tassels at the end of ripe *mealies*, and hung over his forehead down to his eyes. Flicking back some strands, he gave a very slight nod and sat down. Sipho was placed facing him. The boy's thin lips were set downward, and there was something in him that made Sipho feel not just awkward, but uncomfortable.

The smell of chicken, however, soon took over. Everyone's eyes, including Copper's, followed Mama Ada as she carried a large silver plate into the room. The roasted bird surrounded by crisply roasted potatoes was placed in front of Mr. Danny. Sipho's stomach was churning. He could hardly wait to feel the juices in his mouth!

"You can start with that," said Mr. Danny, giving Sipho a plate with a large leg of chicken and two potatoes. "Help yourself to vegetables and gravy."

Following the silence of the first mouthfuls, Judy and Portia began to chat, Mr. Danny joining in at times. Sipho was just wishing he didn't have to struggle with the knife and fork when Mr. Danny said he should use his fingers on the bone. Glancing up, Sipho caught Judy's brother looking straight at him. It wasn't a friendly look. He hardly spoke, even when his father asked him about the rugby match.

"Aw, Dad, I don't want to talk about it."

"I bet that means you lost!" Judy grinned.

Her brother glowered at her but remained silent. He didn't even smile when Mama Ada brought in a large chocolate pudding and ice cream. The only nice thing Sipho saw him do was pass Copper a piece of chicken under the table.

After dinner Judy took Sipho down a long corridor with rooms on either side. There were two sitting rooms.

"We watch television in that one, and this one's the lounge," said Judy. The comfortable-looking sofas were covered in material that looked like a garden of flowers. Dark green curtains hung from the ceiling to the floor along one wall. In one corner stood a piano, and, once again, there were paintings everywhere.

Farther down the corridor, it seemed that everyone in the family had rooms to themselves. Pointing out her father's bedroom, Judy led the way into her own.

"Excuse the mess! Ada's always going on at me!"

Portia was lying on one of two beds with a magazine propped against her knees. She smiled and returned to her reading. Opposite the beds was a stereo system. Tapes, books, and magazines were spread over the floor.

"That's David's room, but he'll shout if we go in. This is where you'll sleep, in here, Sipho."

They had come to a room at the very end of the corridor. Inside, everything was very tidy. Next to the bed was a desk with nothing on it. A single picture hung above the bed. A scene of some trees with flaming red flowers and blue mountains in the distance.

"I bet you'll want to wash off all that horrible lake water," said Judy. "Hold on a minute. I'll be back."

He had seen two bathrooms, one right opposite his room. Judy returned with a large fluffy towel, some pajamas and a pair of smart white *takkies*.

"David has grown out of these pajamas, and I don't use these shoes for tennis anymore. You can have them if they fit."

"I think they will fit. Thank you," said Sipho. The shoes looked almost new.

Watching the steam rising from the water as it ran into the bath, Sipho wondered how much he should take. When you had to carry water a long way from a tap, you only took what you needed. Would anyone be listening to see how long he left the taps on? He didn't think so. But still he didn't like to waste water. When the bath was a quarter full he turned the taps off.

As he stretched out in the hot water, his mind flooded with pictures. Gogo bathing him in a small tub in the yard when he was little. Being rubbed and hugged afterward. Jabu grinning and splashing his head with water under the railway tap. Ducking his own head under and seeing his *malunde* friends through a cascade of icy-cold water. His body hitting the freezing lake, feeling like it was splintering.

Later, lying under the covers in bed, he imagined the places where his friends might be sleeping. Had Lucas found another hideout under a staircase, in an alleyway or another empty plot? The faint sound of music, beating from Judy's stereo down the corridor, reminded him of a song he had heard coming a few times from clubs and cafés in Hillbrow. It would be cold out there. Mr. Danny and Judy had been very kind to him. But he could tell that David

wasn't happy about him. And Mama Ada . . .
once she started asking him questions, she was
bound to find out the truth. That he wasn't
really an orphan. What if they found out he had
a mother and stepfather? What then?

Sipho turned in the bed and buried his face in
the pillow. The other day Jabu had told him
about ostriches and how they buried their heads
in the sand.

"Hey, they're stupid, man! They must leave
their brains in the sand!" Sipho had joked.

But now he wished he could do the same. If
only he could forget all the disturbing thoughts
that jostled in his head.

13. A World Away

⟨※⟩⟨◇⟩⟨※⟩

When he woke, the wall opposite the window was slashed with a strip of bright sunlight. Not sure what to do, Sipho lay in bed, enjoying its softness and listening to the sounds of the house. It was very quiet. Quiet enough to hear birds calling and answering each other outside. Every now and again a dog barked somewhere in the distance. There was no sound, even of motor cars. Perhaps because it was Sunday. Sunday mornings in the township were usually quieter too than weekdays. But even then, when he lay waking on the mattress on the floor of the shack, before long there would always be sounds of someone doing something. A baby crying, a voice calling, a dog barking or whining, someone shouting at it to shut up, a rooster squawking . . .

He had closed his eyes again, trying to make out how many kinds of birds there were outside from their different calls, when he heard a shuffling sound at his door. At first he was puzzled, half expecting the door to open, until he realized who it was. Copper! Slipping out of bed, he went to let him in. In the beam of sunlight, Copper's silky hair seemed even more reddish golden than the night before.

"*Sawubona*, Copper!" whispered Sipho. "You're a good dog."

Copper's large eyes looked up as if they understood, while Sipho stroked him and scratched behind his ears. Sitting on the edge of the bed, with Copper relaxing beside him, Sipho began to feel he had a friend he could trust. When Judy put her head around the door a little later to ask if he would like some breakfast, she smiled.

"Copper must really like you! He doesn't usually take to strangers that easily."

But while Copper's eyes made him feel safe, Mama Ada's made him feel nervous, and it wasn't long before she had the opportunity to question him. He had brought his empty porridge bowl to her at the sink, when she said to him, "Tell me about yourself, Sipho. How do you come to be on the streets?"

"I was with my grandmother, Mama. She worked for the white farmer. Then she died."

"So who took care of you?"

As he looked downward at the zigzag tiles on the floor, his mind raced crazily. He didn't want to lie, but what could he do?

"My mother . . . she brought me here. But then she got very sick, Mama." His voice had gone down to almost a whisper, and he paused. No, he couldn't bring himself to say the actual words that his mother had died. That would be very bad. Instead he wiped his eyes with his hand.

"There was no one to look after me . . . and there was too much fighting and killing in that place. That's why I came to town."

"Where did your mother live?" Mama Ada asked.

Again Sipho panicked. He had to name a different place.

"It was Phola Park, Mama."

Mama Ada was silent. Phola Park was well known. Thousands of people without homes had made shacks for themselves there.

"That place is not good for a child . . . even if a child has his mother," she said, shaking her head and turning back to the sink to continue washing. Pointing to a towel, she asked Sipho to help dry the dishes.

It wasn't clear whether Mama Ada believed him or not. He wondered what she would say to Mr. Danny. But Mr. Danny had already left the house. Judy said that he played golf every Sunday. A little later Mama Ada also left the house. She had prepared some food for them and announced that she would see them in the morning.

"Ada's going to see her children. They're all grown up, so she usually only goes home at weekends," Judy explained to Sipho after Mama Ada had said good-bye.

"Where do they live?" asked Sipho.

"Oh, somewhere in Soweto."

He was relieved. Mama Ada didn't come from his township, then.

"Ada's been with us since I was a baby. She's amazing and so wise. She helped bring me and David up as well as all her own five kids, single-handed. You should ask her how she got rid of her drunken husband! She's really proud about it!"

Sipho didn't know what to say. He was interested in what Judy was saying, but he wasn't used to this way of talking. The way she called Mama Ada by her first name didn't seem respectful. It reminded him of Kobus calling Gogo—who was old enough to be Kobus's grandmother—"Sarah." But at the same time Judy really seemed to like Mama Ada. If Mama Ada was also so wise, like Judy said, he would have to be very careful not to give her any clues that would show up his lies.

Sipho spent most of the day watching television, listening to music and playing cards with the two girls. Judy's brother seemed to be keeping away from them, staying in his room. When a friend of his came over, instead of inviting the boy in they heard David suggest they go out to visit another friend. Sipho saw how Portia raised her eyebrows and Judy shrugged in return. They didn't say anything. Did David's behavior have something to do with him? Sipho caught sight of the two boys as they walked out of the driveway. The friend was white, and both boys' heads were bent in close conversation. Were they talking about him?

In the late afternoon, just before setting off with her father to take Portia home, Judy brought Sipho a handful of old comics. Absorbed in the adventures of Batman, he hardly noticed that David had come into the sitting room until the television came on with a blast. Copper, who had been sleeping on the floor next to Sipho, jumped up with a bark and padded across to David, his tail wagging. Without saying anything, David threw himself onto the sofa in front of the screen, scratching Copper behind the ears in the same place Sipho had done.

That evening, however, at the table, David suddenly accused Judy of stealing his comics from the bookcase outside his room.

"Come off it, Dave! It's not stealing just to take a few old comics to read!" Judy laughed.

Sipho felt the heat rising to his face.

"Stop it, you two!" said Mr. Danny, raising his voice. "What's this all about?"

"Dave is getting paranoid because I borrowed some of his old comics for Sipho."

"You didn't ask me," David blurted out.

"You weren't here to ask! What's your problem? Sipho's only reading them. He's not *eating* them!" retorted Judy.

"Well, I'm not going to have any arguments at the dinner table, least of all on a Sunday, the one day I have to rest," Mr. Danny stated severely.

Judy and David glared at each other but kept quiet. Sipho sat embarrassed. Judy was right. He hadn't eaten the comics! They were safe in the next room. Her brother must be angry about something else. Whatever it was, it was probably something to do with him.

"You will need to be ready by quarter to seven tomorrow morning, Sipho." Mr. Danny's voice interrupted his thoughts. "That's the time we leave for the shop, all right?"

"Yes, sir," he replied. "I'll be ready."

He wanted to ask whether Mr. Danny would bring him back to his home again the next evening, but it didn't seem to be the right time.

"I trust you two have done all your homework for tomorrow," Mr. Danny said, getting up from the table. His eyes were on his son.

"Yes, Dad," David replied in a bored voice, as if words had to be dragged from his mouth.

Like the night before, Sipho didn't fall asleep immediately. Once again, too many thoughts were whirling through his head. Among them was Mr. Danny talking about homework. For a whole week he had hardly thought about his own school. Who had missed him there? With nearly seventy children in the class, he might have hoped to escape unnoticed by the teacher. But not with his teacher. She took a roll call every day and was very strict. By the end of the week she would surely have asked why he wasn't there. Would Gordon have said anything? Or had Ma been up to the school?

In this soft, warm bed it felt like he was a world away from Gordon, Ma, and his life in the township. Yet it was only a taxi ride away. Even nearer were Jabu and the rest of the gang . . . somewhere out there in the cold of Hillbrow. But from this bed here in Mr. Danny's house, it felt like he was a world away from them too.

14. On Edge

✕◇✕◇✕

On Monday, Sipho was either advertising T-shirts at the corner or minding the front of the shop to see that no one stole anything from the tables. When Mr. Danny said he could break for lunch, Sipho told him that he wanted to look for his friends. None of them had come past on their way to the video shop.

"Just make sure you're back in an hour," Mr. Danny warned. "By the way, Maria's made you a sandwich. You'd better take it with you."

Mr. Danny was puzzling. One minute he seemed ready to jump down his throat, the next he was taking care of him. Biting off mouthfuls of sandwich as he ran, Sipho darted along the pavement, in and out of shoppers and pavement sellers, making his way to Checkers. He was nearly there when he caught sight of Joseph and Jabu in a side street "parking" a car. Sipho called out and waited for them to finish. Wasn't this near the place he had seen them the first time—

only a week ago? Joseph still had his army jacket, but this time he had a woolen hat pulled down to his eyebrows. He greeted Sipho but didn't smile.

"*Heyta, buti!* Where have you been? We thought you might have been kidnapped!" At least Jabu seemed really pleased to see him.

Sipho grinned. "What made you think that?"

Someone from another gang, explained Jabu, had seen Sipho standing at the corner and shouting about Danny's Den. Someone else thought they had seen him in the back of a car being driven by a white man. Then when he didn't appear again, they began to wonder what had happened.

Sipho told his story, adding that he still wasn't sure whether Mr. Danny would take him home again that night. He was waiting to see. But what had happened to the gang?

"What do you think? When you were in your nice bed, we were still on the street!" There was a note of roughness in Joseph's voice.

"Cool it, Joe!" said Jabu, putting his hand on Joseph's shoulder. The last two nights had been spent in a small yard at the back of a drugstore. It kept them out of the wind at least. The problem was that they had to be out of there before the manager arrived in the morning.

"Lucas is looking for a new place for us. Maybe he'll find something good," said Jabu hopefully.

There was no sign of the others outside Checkers, and it was soon time for Sipho to get back to Danny's Den. Joseph laughed that Sipho was worried about being late.

"Me, I like my freedom, man! Right now, I feel like a rest. So I take it!"

He slid down to the pavement, his back against the Checkers wall with one hand resting on the familiar bulge in his pocket.

"I'll walk with you," offered Jabu. "I can show you where we have our *pozzie.*"

Something in Joseph's manner had warned Sipho off asking him about *iglue* in his hair. He had taken note of the cap.

"He doesn't like people to see his head now," said Jabu. He made quick snipping movements with two fingers around Sipho's head. "Some of them laugh and call him '*cheesekop.*' The barber shaved off all his hair!"

It was the same for Matthew. When the *iglue* wouldn't wash out, they had looked for a barber. Some chased them away because *malunde* sometimes annoyed their customers, making fun of unusual styles. However, this barber had been shocked by their story, and he didn't even charge them. But while Matthew now joked about his head as smooth as a piece of cheese, Joseph was still very upset.

They were just a couple of blocks away from

Danny's Den when two angry voices rose above the hum of the street. Seeing a small crowd gathered nearby, the boys made their way into it.

"You always follow me and I'm sick of it! Can't you leave me alone!"

A very young woman with heavy makeup, swinging earrings, a shiny red blouse and a short black skirt was shouting in a high voice at an older man in a pale blue suit. He was short and fat, with his arms folded, although his small, piercing eyes suggested that his arms were ready to swipe out at any moment.

"You promise to meet me and then you don't turn up! You need to be taught a lesson you won't forget."

The man's voice was a growl. It brought back horrible memories for Sipho. Since he had come to live in the township he had also seen this kind of argument between a man and a woman. He knew what was going to happen, and it would be upsetting to watch. This young woman was hardly more than a girl, about as old as Lucas. Mr. Danny would also be angry if he was late. Tapping his friend on the arm, he signaled goodbye and slipped out between the onlookers.

"I'll come and see you," Jabu called after him. He was staying to watch the whole scene develop.

Mr. Danny took Sipho home with him that

evening—and the one after that and the one after that. Nothing was directly said. But every evening Sipho swept, and sometimes washed, the shop floor while Mr. Danny worked in the office. And every evening when Mr. Danny had finished, he would look out of the office door and say, "Okay, Sipho? Ready to go?"

At the house, Mama Ada and Copper would greet them at the door. Copper would bark, wag his tail and rub up against them. Even if she was busy with her homework, Judy would still call out "Hello." Mama Ada would ask him about his day and he would answer her, trying to remember not to let his conversation become too free in case he let out something that uncovered his true past. Only David remained very withdrawn, hardly speaking to Sipho at all. What made Sipho feel more awkward was that Mr. Danny had given him some clothes David had grown out of—some of them still quite new. But the way David looked at him, without saying anything, made Sipho feel like he had no right to them . . . almost like he was a thief.

Some evenings, instead of watching television, Judy would take out cards or a board game for them to play. Occasionally Mr. Danny joined in, but mostly it was Judy and Sipho. She asked him about his schooling, and he told her that he had made it to grade two. Judy offered to help him, finding a couple of old grade two math and English books. They had belonged to David, who was now in grade four. But by nighttime, after a full day's work, Sipho found it hard to concentrate on schoolwork, so the lesson was never for very long.

David stayed in his room when he wasn't watching the television or using it for his video games. One night, however, at the end of Sipho's first week, he seemed in a better mood than usual and invited his father to try his video speed-racing game.

"I'll have to practice secretly so I beat you one of these days!" laughed Mr. Danny as his final score came up on the screen. "Here, Sipho, why don't you have a go?" Mr. Danny held out the controls, offering them to Sipho. But as he took them, David stormed out of the room, banging the door. Copper, whose sleep had been disturbed, jumped up and sniffed at the door.

"David, come back!" called Mr. Danny, but there was no response.

Sipho tried to concentrate on the game while father and daughter spoke in lowered voices. Then Mr. Danny left the room, and Sipho put the game down. He wasn't enjoying it at all.

"I'll go to bed," he told Judy.

"Sipho, you must try not to mind David." Her

voice was apologetic. "Since Mum left home last year, he's been really difficult. He's lost his temper with everyone, even Ada."

"He doesn't like me," Sipho stated simply.

"At the moment he doesn't like anyone," replied Judy.

He was reaching out to the door handle when Judy said, "You see, David was always Mum's little boy . . ."

On the last three words, her voice suddenly wavered and stopped. She usually sounded so confident about everything. Sipho turned around to face her. She was twisting some long strands of hair around her finger.

"When she and I had rows even over silly little things, David always used to take Mum's side. And then when the big rows started between her and Dad, he used to blame Dad. That's why it was such a shock for him when she left . . ."

There was another pause.

"I bet her boyfriend didn't want David tagging along when they went off to Cape Town . . . David wouldn't even speak to Mum on the phone when she rang. Dad just buries himself in his work now, and I tend to get on with things. But David still shows the hurt."

Sipho didn't know what to say, and luckily it seemed that Judy didn't expect a reply. Running her fingers through her hair, she suddenly seemed to be embarrassed.

"Oh, I'm sorry, Sipho, to have gone on for so long about our problems. I forgot that you know what it's like to lose your mother and everything."

Sipho bit on his lip and said goodnight.

Throughout the next day, while he worked at the shop, Sipho's mind kept coming back to what Judy had told him, especially her statement "You must try not to mind David." But when David looked at him like he was a piece of dirt, it hurt. Judy had said her brother was angry with everyone. Sipho remembered the rage he had felt the last time his stepfather had beaten him. He had cut himself off for days from everyone then. Was that how it was with David? But he, Sipho, had been filled with anger because his stepfather was brutal, beating him for no reason, and his mother wouldn't—or couldn't—protect him. David wasn't being beaten. And didn't he have almost everything he wanted in this house? Except his mother. His mother had chosen someone else instead of him. That hurt. He knew . . .

But then there was also the way David flinched slightly any time Sipho went past. As if Sipho might give him some disease. Whatever David's reasons, he left Sipho feeling bad. David forced him to remember that he didn't really belong with this family.

It seemed he didn't belong with the *malunde* either anymore. He had seen some members of the gang once or twice during his midday break or when they passed Danny's Den on the way to the video shop. Jabu had come by a few times specially. But their time together was always short, and Mr. Danny didn't like people coming into the shop if they weren't going to buy anything. What Sipho missed was being free to go around together, to chat and look at things in the streets, without being rushed. He had only once been able to check during the week to see that the little wooden rhino was still for sale. He had found it again, looking at him with its worried eye.

"I'll come and get you one day soon, don't worry!" he had whispered under his breath.

But Mr. Danny hadn't given him any money yet, and he was unsure about asking. Maybe Mr. Danny was going to give him wages at the end of the month like an adult worker? Or maybe . . . he wouldn't get anything because he was staying and eating in Mr. Danny's house now.

But in the meantime, he wasn't Mr. Danny's prisoner, was he? At least he could spend Sunday with his friends—and be out of David's way. Sipho began to plan his day off.

15. Friendship

>※>※<>※<

M r. Danny and Judy seemed a little surprised when Sipho announced on Saturday night that he would be going out to see his friends the next day. David, as usual, just stared at him, although this time Sipho thought there was a flicker of curiosity in his eyes.

"Portia's coming around tomorrow. It was fun last week when you were here too," said Judy.

But Sipho had made up his mind, and he wasn't put off by the thought of walking all the way to Hillbrow.

"You must be back by seven-thirty at the latest, mind. Otherwise you'll have us all worried," Mr. Danny said firmly, raising one eyebrow.

Sipho wondered how he did that.

"Yes, sir," he replied.

He didn't have a watch, but if he started walking back from Hillbrow at the time the sun began to go down, he would be all right.

. . . . . .

Sipho intended to get to the gang's new *pozzie* when they would be waking up. As he opened the front door early on Sunday morning while the rest of the house was still all quiet, Copper wagged his tail excitedly. He thought Sipho was going to take him for a walk. Mr. Danny usually ran around a few blocks with Copper galloping beside him early in the morning.

"No, Copper, you can't come with me," Sipho whispered. "Mr. Danny will take you later."

Slipping through the door, he closed it swiftly behind him with Copper looking sorrowful. Only as the latch clicked did he remember that the gate was locked and that the button to open it was inside the house. The gate and the walls were high. He could try to climb them, but what if someone outside saw him and thought he was a burglar? If he rang the bell, that would wake Mr. Danny. Sipho began to think he would just have to wait a while, when he remembered Mama Ada. There was a chance that she might be up, if he went to her room around the back of the house.

Mama Ada was indeed awake and had already washed and dressed.

"I always get up at five. Even Sundays, so I can leave early to see my children," she told Sipho as she opened the back door to the house with her key. "You know, I miss my children even now they are big! It's the same with every mother."

Why did she say this to him? He wasn't going to let himself fall into a trap.

"But, Mama, why did Mr. Danny's wife leave her children?"

"*Hawu*, Sipho! That question is too difficult. I don't like to think of it. When I see Judy and David and think of their mother, my heart is very sore. When David was small, he was such a happy little boy."

Mama Ada didn't say any more. But before she pressed the button for the gate, she told Sipho to take care and to be sure to return by the time Mr. Danny had said.

"You have a roof over your head and food in your stomach in this house, my child," she added.

Could Mama Ada have sensed some of his thoughts, wondered Sipho? He set off at a jog down the tree-lined street, and his mind was soon racing ahead to the different things he and his friends might do together during the day.

It wasn't as he had imagined it would be. When he arrived in the alleyway at the back of the drugstore, there was no sound coming from the *pozzie*. When Jabu had brought him past here before, he had noted that the drugstore's wall was not quite as high as the others, but it was still taller than he was. Finding a broken brick for one foot, Sipho heaved himself up. The whole gang was still sound asleep in a heap in the far corner! He had forgotten that the shop didn't open on Sunday and so they wouldn't need to get up until later. They had probably only gone to sleep after the Saturday late-night crowds had gone home. Swinging himself over, he dropped down quietly and sat in one corner. The cold rose through the concrete floor. With tall buildings all around, the early-morning sun didn't reach the yard. Time seemed to pass slowly. If only Jabu had been lying on the outside of the pile of *malunde*, Sipho might have tried waking him without disturbing the others. But Jabu was tucked right in the middle of everyone.

The sun was high when the gang woke up. No one seemed particularly surprised to see Sipho sitting there. Even Jabu was still half asleep at first and just nodded his greeting between yawns.

"Did your new boss give you the sack?" Joseph wanted to know.

When Sipho explained he had come just for the day, Joseph lost interest. A little later as they were walking to the main street, Lucas asked Sipho about Mr. Danny. Was there any place for a *pozzie* at the back of his shop and was he friendly? Sipho explained that the yard at Danny's Den was completely closed in. And although Mr. Danny had taken him in to work for him, he didn't like *malunde* hanging around in front of his shop.

The gang spread themselves out between a restaurant, a café, and a take-out shop. Sipho stood with them, putting out his hands when a customer walked by. Not having eaten since the night before, he was also hungry. But when Vusi asked him if he ate roast meat every day with Mr. Danny, although he said "no," he suddenly felt guilty. When he went back to Mr. Danny's home, there would be a meal waiting for him—as much as he wanted to eat. What surprised the others, however, was that Sipho didn't have any money with him.

"You must be hiding it, man! How can you work for that white man and he doesn't pay you?" Joseph was disbelieving and his hoarse voice cut into Sipho.

"He gives me food and clothes. It's only money he doesn't give. But I think he'll give it to me at the end of the month," explained Sipho.

"Hey, that's funny. You didn't ask? What kind of boss is it who doesn't give money?" Joseph shook his head and made a face. He seemed to be suggesting that Sipho was either a liar or stupid.

"*Ja*, you must ask your boss," Vusi added casually. "Everyone has to pay."

Sipho didn't like the way Vusi was looking at him, and he was grateful that Lucas was nearby.

Later on, the gang decided to go to Parktown. They would spend the rest of the afternoon at the Zoo Lake and "ask money" from people having an afternoon out. There might even be a chance to slip into the zoo itself. Sipho wanted to go too, but it was in the other direction from Mr. Danny's house and he was worried that he would not be back in time.

"When you are *malunde*, you are free!" Joseph laughed openly.

It was tempting to go along with them. Sipho had never been to a zoo before. Would it matter so much if he was a bit late? But before he could say anything, Jabu announced that he was staying behind in Hillbrow. There was a film he wanted to see at the *bhiyo*. He was friendly with the person on the door for the afternoon show, and if it wasn't full up she would sneak Jabu and Sipho in.

The film had lots of shooting and fast cars chasing each other. Jabu's friend, the attendant, had whispered to them to go to the very front row. They were so close to the screen it was almost like they were in the action themselves. Sipho and Jabu gripped their seats as their car hurtled full-speed around the sharp bends of a narrow mountain road. Each time it nearly went over the edge, they gritted their teeth. Finally, when the car chasing them crashed and burst into flames, they cheered with others in the audience.

When it was all over, they walked out arm in arm into the street. Sipho could tell from the pink light that it was nearly time for him to go. But he held back. He was enjoying himself here in Hillbrow.

"It's true what Joseph said. When you are *malunde* you're free," he said to Jabu.

Jabu made a sucking sound, drawing air in through his teeth. "Joseph talks that way because he's jealous! When he's sleeping on the cold ground, you are sleeping in a warm bed and when he's hungry, you have hot food inside you."

That was very true. But it was also true that he, Sipho, wasn't free. It was hard to put into words, but he began to tell Jabu about Mr. Danny's family. While he knew Mr. Danny was trying to help him, his son, David, made him feel very uncomfortable. He couldn't ever really belong to Mr. Danny's family, could he? So shouldn't he just join the gang of *malunde* again?

Jabu interrupted him. Sipho was surely crazy. Didn't he see that the boy David was *trying* to make him leave? Why should he give up every-thing just because of him? And had he forgot-ten all the bad things . . . the cold winds at night . . . searching always for money and food . . . not being safe and being attacked?

"If it was me, I would be happy to stay with Mr. Danny," he declared.

Sipho was quiet. Jabu was right, of course, and sensible. But still he didn't understand how he, Sipho, felt.

"Well, I have to go," he said finally.

He was pleased when Jabu began to walk with him. It was rapidly getting dark, and he expected his friend to turn back once they reached the end of Hillbrow, but Jabu walked on. They were so busy talking, kicking an empty can along the pavement and still talking, that almost before Sipho realized it they had walked all the way to the street where Mr. Danny's house was. Suddenly he felt very bad. He was going to go inside, and Jabu was going to be left outside. It had been fun walking together, but now Jabu would have to walk back to Hillbrow by himself. Perhaps he could come inside first to have some-thing to drink? If Judy opened the door he felt sure that would be all right. But as he pressed the button on the box by the gate, he noticed that Mr. Danny's car was out of the garage. He and Judy must have gone to take Portia home.

"Who is it?" David's voice came sharply out of the box.

"It's me, Sipho."

There was no reply, but after a few moments the iron gate began to move slowly aside. There was no point in asking Jabu to come with him. David would say bluntly that he wasn't allowed to let strangers into the house, and that would be even worse.

Sipho stepped inside the drive, and he and Jabu stood on opposite sides as the gate began to slide back again.

"Hey, these people have all kinds of smart things!" Jabu's large, dark eyes followed the movement. "It's like there's a spook pushing it!" he added.

They both laughed. Then Sipho heard the front door click open behind him. David must be there watching them. He looked through the iron bars at his friend shut out on the other side. He could see that Jabu's eyes had wandered in the direction of the door.

"We'll meet soon," said Jabu. "*Sala kahle.*"

"Yes, I shall come to look for you. *Hamba kahle,*" Sipho replied.

For a few moments he watched the figure of his friend as it slipped from a patch of light under a streetlamp into a stretch of darkness. Then he turned to face the house.

16. Accused!

XOXOXOXO

The days followed in the same pattern as his first week at Mr. Danny's. Six long days of working in the shop with only Sunday free for a few hours to go looking for his friends. In the evenings David had nothing to do with him and made a point of calling Copper away if he saw him with Sipho. Judy remained very friendly, while Mama Ada also took an interest in him. She was especially pleased whenever she saw Judy helping him at night with some writing.

"It's good. You must study hard. Then you can be someone in life," she commented as she cleared the dishes from the table.

But Sipho continued to be tired by the evening and not able to take much in. The work at Danny's Den became harder and his time off at midday shorter after Mr. Danny had an argument with Maria. It was about her being late. When Mr. Danny shouted that he was going to take some money off her wages, Maria declared that she wanted to be paid right away. She was leaving. Her brother was getting her a job in a supermarket right near her home. And it was going to be more money. Mr. Danny could keep his job!

"You people are all the same!" Mr. Danny said angrily. "You want something for nothing. You come late but I must pay you. Then you hear about an easier job and you leave."

Sipho was inside the shop, watching the whole scene. Mr. Danny opened the register and flung some notes and a few coins down on the counter in front of her. Catching Sipho's eye, Maria nodded at him grimly. With a loud complaint about bosses who expected you to work for next to nothing, she strode angrily out into the street. Seeing Sipho silently standing there, Mr. Danny suddenly turned on him. His face was still red from the argument, and his mouth and mustache twitched as he spoke sharply.

"What are you doing there, just standing? You'll have to help with Maria's work until I can find someone else!"

By the time they were going home in the car, he seemed a little calmer. He even said that he was sorry for having been short-tempered with Sipho.

"But you know it's not easy to run a shop. There's always something to worry about."

· · · · · ·

It was a few days later that Mr. Danny announced that some of his stock was missing. There had been a delivery of jeans, but some of the batch seemed to be gone. They hadn't been sold—and that could mean only one thing. Mr. Danny questioned Sipho.

"I don't know, Mr. Danny," was all he could say.

But when Mr. Danny started talking about *malunde*, he became worried.

"Are you sure that some of your street friends aren't wearing nice new jeans, Sipho?" The one eyebrow was raised.

Was Mr. Danny accusing him? Of stealing the jeans for his friends? He was almost too shocked to reply. He shook his head fiercely. A lump in his stomach seemed to shoot up to his throat and stick there. At last he swallowed and managed to get out some words.

"How can I do that, sir?"

"Well, it's very strange, Sipho . . . very strange. But I'll get to the bottom of it in the end. I always do."

Mr. Danny's words hung like a threat over Sipho for the rest of the day.

It felt as if Mr. Danny's eyes too were following him everywhere in the shop. Whenever he happened to look in Mr. Danny's direction,

there were the eyes looking at him. As they traveled back to the house after work, Mr. Danny
usually talked. But this evening he remained
completely silent. Mama Ada knew something
was wrong as soon as she opened the door. There
was no "Evening, Ada!" Just a surly glance.
Copper seemed to guess his master's mood too.
His eyes looked doleful and his tail less jaunty as
he rubbed himself up against Sipho's legs.

At dinner, when Judy asked what was wrong,
her father replied in a low, serious tone that some
stock was missing.

"How could that happen, Dad?"

"That's just what I don't know, Jude . . . just
what I don't know."

As he looked up from his plate, Sipho caught
Judy's eyes flicking away from him. He didn't
look at David. He could imagine the fixed stare
and, this time, a sneer.

He went to his bedroom early to avoid being
in the family room with them all. How could he
prove that he knew nothing about the missing
jeans? Judy wouldn't want to believe he was a
thief, but if her father said it was very suspicious,
then what would she think? Once again, he
began to think it would be simplest if he went
back to the streets. But if he went now, they
would all believe he was guilty . . .

Thirsty for a drink of water, he went to the

kitchen. Mama Ada was just preparing to leave but stopped when she saw him.

"What is this I hear, my child?" she said, frowning.

He hoped her deep, searching eyes would know that he was telling the truth as he went over what had happened. Mama Ada sighed.

"In this life there's always trouble. But maybe Mr. Danny will find what he has lost."

Mama Ada was right. When Sipho came into the kitchen for breakfast the next morning, Mr. Danny was at the kitchen table, smiling. He had spent the night checking his papers and found a mistake in his records. There were no jeans missing after all! The delivery had been smaller than what he had ordered, but the full number had still been written in the book. It had happened the day after Maria had left.

"You know, Sipho, my mind must have been really wandering then!" He brushed his mustache with his forefinger. "I have to admit I was very worried that I'd made a big mistake about you. Lots of shopkeepers have stories about street children stealing from them. They would say I was a real fool . . ."

Sipho could tell that Mama Ada was listening as she dished up the porridge behind Mr. Danny. She gave him a wink as she came across to the table, a bowl in each hand. Sipho tried to relax. But inside himself, he felt the knot that had been there all night still tightly twisted. Even Judy's wide-open laugh didn't untwist it.

"Honestly, Dad, you'll really have to watch yourself in your old age! Getting everyone worried like that!"

She turned to Sipho.

"Dad is hardly a brilliant detective, is he?" She grinned.

He could feel she was trying to cheer him up, but it was difficult to respond. Did Judy have any idea what it felt like to be accused of being a thief one minute and then be expected to forget it all the next minute, because it was a mistake?

That evening, when Judy asked if he wanted to do some reading or play cards, he said he was too tired and would go to bed early again. He could tell from her face that she was disappointed. But he wanted to be alone. All day in the shop, he had felt Mr. Danny was trying to be nice to him. He had even sent him to buy burgers and chips for them at midday. What he needed, however, was time to think. The one person he would like to talk to wasn't even able to come into Danny's Den, let alone Mr. Danny's house.

17. No Turning Back

```
░░░░░░░░░░
```

When he turned on the light in the bedroom, the first thing that caught Sipho's eye was a folded piece of paper propped up on the desk next to his bed. In large letters was written the word THIEF. The pile of old grade two books that had belonged to David—which he kept on the desk—was also missing.

His first instinct was to tear the note up. The anger hidden deep inside when Mr. Danny suspected him now wanted to burst out. But no, he wouldn't tear the paper up. He would go and face them all with it. Let David explain in front of them all what he meant. He was sick and tired of David looking at him like he was a nothing . . . a piece of dirt . . . and now a thief.

With the paper in his hand, Sipho hurried back down the corridor toward the family room. The door was slightly open, and he was about to push it when he stopped himself. An argument was going on, and he heard his name. Judy was saying something about him.

"It's not right, Dad! Kids of his age should be in school! Like me and Dave."

Her voice was determined.

"He could work in the shop *after* school and on the weekend," she added.

"Look here, Judy, I can't—and you can't—sort out the world's problems. There are dozens of street kids. Next thing you'll be saying I must get them into school too."

"No, I'm not. I'm talking about Sipho."

Sipho could imagine Judy's deep blue eyes steadily fixed on her father's face.

"He should be grateful just to have a job and a roof over his head. Have you forgotten the state he was in when I took him in?"

Sipho clenched his fists, crumpling the paper. He listened as Mr. Danny started talking about how he had left school at fourteen. "I was buying and selling when I was hardly older than Sipho. You forget that. I'd gone bust three times before I was twenty!"

"But at least you could read and write properly before you left school, Dad."

"Listen. I'm giving that boy a chance to learn something about business. And if he wants to succeed, he'll succeed!"

"Then why don't you pull Dave out of school and let him do the same?"

"For God's sake, Jude, there's a difference. David is my son. I'm just giving Sipho a helping hand. You need to get it into your head that I'm not running a full-scale charity!"

There was silence in the room. Sipho held his breath. Was there any point in going in?

"You, my dear Judy, might enjoy being Miss Lady Charity, but as far as I'm concerned Sipho is another employee to me—"

"So what do you pay him then, Dad?" interrupted Judy.

"Isn't it enough that he's being better fed and looked after than he's been in his whole life? And if David, my own son, continues to be unhappy with him here, then something will have to be done."

Sipho didn't want to hear any more. All this pretense of being a friend was just a lie of Mr. Danny's. What was the point in staying? Mr. Danny was going to throw him out anyway. He would rather leave himself. He flung down the crushed paper in his hand. It landed in the middle of the hallway with the offensive word staring upward through the creases. Tears were blurring the pattern on the red carpet as he darted to the door. Lifting the chain, he pulled and tugged at the handle. Cold air hit him in the face. He needed to dash to the bedroom to collect his jacket, but at that moment he heard Mr.

Danny's voice coming closer. They were coming out of the family room. He didn't want to see them, not even Judy. She would insist that he must stay, and there would be a scene. With a quick jab at the gate button, he slipped out and pulled the heavy door shut behind him. His heart was doing its puppy-dog thumping as he ran toward the gate. Copper was barking behind the front door. He would have liked to stroke him one last time to say goodbye.

Once past the moving gate, Sipho was absorbed into the darker shadows of the road. Above him the leaves in the trees were fluttering wildly. He was running as fast as he could, the wind biting right through his sweater into his skin. A sudden spate of barks from behind a high wall made him flinch and cross to the other side of the road. His own rapid breaths seemed to pound in his ears. When he heard his name being called by a girl's voice in the distance behind him, it already seemed to come from a world away. A minute later, the sound of a car approaching made him turn and strain his eyes against the headlights. Was it Mr. Danny? Were they coming after him? But the car whisked by, its red tail lights disappearing down the road ahead. Once again, he was quite alone.

Around the corner, something came flying toward his face. He put out his hand. Just a plastic bag whipped up by the wind. The last time he remembered the wind as fierce as this, Ma had been worried that the sheet of iron covering their home would be blown away. It was only held down by a few heavy stones. He and Ma had searched through their belongings for something else heavy to put on the roof, but there was nothing. His stepfather was out, as usual. The two of them had sat close together on the bed, listening to the wind shaking and rattling everything around them.

He could even remember the story Ma had told him about the wind and the sun having a contest to show which was stronger. The wind had lost in Ma's story. With it raging all around them at the time, he had thought Ma had made her story up to make him feel better. And then all of a sudden everything had gone quiet and they had both gone to sleep, Ma in her bed and he on his mattress on the floor. But later, when his stepfather had returned, it was like being waked up by a whirlwind raging inside the room instead of outside.

Sipho's mind returned to that night as, now running, now jogging, now walking—sometimes partly pushed by the wind, sometimes struggling against it—he weaved his way back toward Hillbrow. What was Ma doing tonight? Was she sitting on the bed all by herself, listening to the wind tugging at the roof? What if it succeeded and the metal sheet went flying off, sending the stones clattering down? What then? And what . . . Sipho blocked off his mind. He needed to concentrate on getting across a main road wide enough for three lanes of cars traveling in each direction. But once he was on the other side, still pushing himself against the wind, a picture forced itself clearly into his mind. What if Ma's baby had arrived by now and Ma was left cradling the baby while the shack crashed down all around her? Who would be there to help?

No, he couldn't worry about that. It wasn't his problem. He needed to attend to finding Jabu and the others—and somewhere to sleep for the night. He couldn't have chosen a worse night to leave Mr. Danny's. But then he hadn't stopped to think whether it was a sensible thing to do. It was a bit like running away the first time. Something inside him had just said he must do it—and that was it.

With the wind so strong, there were fewer people than usual out on the streets leading up to Hillbrow. Jabu and the others would surely have already set themselves up for the night at the back of the drugstore, huddling together to keep warm. Tomorrow he would have to go to Rosebank to earn enough money to buy another jacket. Perhaps Jabu would come with him again.

Arriving at Checkers, Sipho looked for the gang of *malunde* who usually made their fire on the opposite pavement. But they were not there tonight. It must have been too windy for them. Walking down the street, he glanced at everyone he passed. Two children were crouched in a shop doorway, but he didn't recognize them. Seeing ahead of him a couple of adults covered with a blanket, he stepped out into the road so as not to pass by too close. Coming at last to the block with the drugstore, Sipho made his way to the back alley. He had only been there in the daytime before. There had been nothing frightening about it then. But tonight, with the streetlight only reaching the entrance, it looked very dark, long and lonely.

To get to the *pozzie* meant passing by a number of other backyards. Biting his lower lip, Sipho entered the narrow passage. The smell of rotting food made him hold his nose. He wanted to run ahead to get away from it but, not able to see where he was going, he stubbed his toe against something and almost tripped. Trying to adjust his eyes to the dimness ahead, he wondered if he should call out. If the gang was still awake, he would hear their voices and, with luck, see flickering sparks from a fire. But ahead there was only darkness and complete quiet. Surely they hadn't already gone to sleep? Putting out his right hand to feel the height of the backyard walls and find the one that was a little lower, Sipho edged his way forward.

Reaching it, he called softly. "Jabu? Lucas? Joseph?"

There was no reply—and no sound or sign of any fire. Quickly he began to feel around the brickwork for the hole that would give him a foothold. Finding it, he swung himself up and peered over the wall. Even in the darkness he could tell that the yard was completely empty.

He stood there suspended for a few moments, wondering what to do. Should he climb into the yard and stay there, hoping the others would return? It would be very cold and very scary on his own. What if they had gone back to the first *pozzie*? To get there he would have to walk by the park where the *tsotsi* gangsters hung out. He didn't like that. Perhaps he would walk a bit through Hillbrow and, if he didn't find the gang there, he would come back to the yard a little later.

He was getting down from the wall when suddenly he was aware that someone else was in the alley. A match was struck, and in that split second of flickering light he sensed a large figure looming toward him with something glinting in its hand.

"Come here, you!"

Sipho leaped and ran.

18. The Garbage Can

Bursting out of the alley, he darted up toward the main street and the lights, glancing back only as he turned the corner. To his horror, the figure was still coming. Heavily built and with a broken bottle in one hand. On the pavement ahead, a man and woman holding hands moved quickly aside. Sipho saw the startled looks on their faces. There was no time to stop and ask for help. And who would help anyway?

He was coming to the shopping mall. In the daytime it was full of stalls and traders. Now the place was dark inside, silent and empty. Was there anywhere to hide? Without thinking he dashed in, throwing himself under the stairs, behind a garbage can. A few seconds later he heard the heavy running footsteps come to a halt. The man had stopped. If he looked under the stairs first of all, that would be it.

"Come out, you little cheat! Pay me what you owe me."

The man was out of breath, and his words had the rasping sound of an unsteady saw cutting through wood. He must have mistaken Sipho for someone else! Pressing himself hard against the cold concrete, Sipho closed his eyes and prayed. If only he could make himself like stone, all the churning and pounding inside his body would stop.

There were footsteps above him. The man was going up the stairs to look around the top. Soon he would be down again. If Sipho ran out now he would see him. There was only one possible way out. The garbage can next to him. Raising himself up, he carefully opened the lid. It was too dark to see inside, but, using his hand, he felt that it wasn't full. Gritting his teeth, he lifted one leg over the edge. He felt something squashing down underneath his foot. Bringing over the second leg and crouching down as small as he could, he gently brought the lid down on top of himself. He clenched his hand over his mouth to stop himself from feeling sick.

Squatting tightly inside the garbage can, Sipho listened intently to the sounds from outside. Everything seemed quiet for a short while. Matthew and Thabo had talked about sleeping in garbage cans. He remembered how he had laughed when they said that people threw rubbish on top of them sometimes.

The footsteps returned, along with rough shouting and swearing. The voice seemed to be circling the stairs and the can. It was complaining about the boy taking his goods to sell and disappearing. Suddenly Sipho realized who this man probably was. A drug dealer who had confused him with one of the boys he used. That meant big trouble. He cringed lower into the can.

When everything went still outside, Sipho was left trapped. Had the man left? He might just be sitting quietly at the bottom of the steps. It was too dangerous to open the lid. Fortunately a tiny bit of air came in where the lid didn't fit closely. But he was so uncomfortable and achingly cold. He would just have to stay there. Where else could he go anyway? He pictured his warm bed, empty, in Mr. Danny's house. And then the word THIEF staring at him from the table. He could hear Mr. Danny's voice: "He should be grateful just to have a job and a roof over his head . . ." He could picture Judy arguing with her father. She had tried hard to be friendly. But it was very difficult. He could imagine Mama Ada shaking her head and saying how foolish he was to run away. Even people who wanted to help him didn't know how he felt. The only friend he could really trust was Jabu . . .

Sipho's mind covered so many thoughts that

night that he wasn't sure when he had fallen asleep and begun to dream. At one point, running away in terror from someone with a shadowy face, he tripped. A sharp object ready to strike him suddenly changed into a horn, and he found himself looking instead into the eyes of his little rhino! Gently it nudged him up, but then another figure with a weapon loomed up behind them, and both he and the rhino were being chased. Just as he was about to try and jump onto the animal's back, it disappeared, and in its place was a rumbling, roaring *gumba-gumba*. He was trapped . . .

When light began to poke through the slit between the lid and the can, Sipho decided to push up the lid. His body was so cramped that it was painful lifting himself up. He managed it as quietly as he could. Stepping out, he could see no sign of the man with the broken bottle. Limping in the direction of Checkers, he kept a sharp lookout for him.

If he stayed by Checkers, sooner or later someone from the gang was sure to come by. He was the first *malunde* at the store and sat down outside, waiting. When the doors opened he stood by, ready to push *amatrolley*. Sipho wasn't sure whether the pain in his stomach came from the remains of his fright or hunger, but by the middle of the morning he had earned enough for some bread and milk. Other *malunde* came and went but no one from his gang.

It was after midday and he was beginning to wonder whether he should start scouring the streets, when he spotted Joseph coming across the road. He seemed slightly unsteady and his one hand remained fixed in his pocket. Sipho saw the usual bulge.

"Hey, your boss is calling you! I can hear him in here." Joseph pointed to his ear. "He wants you to hurry," Joseph added, grinning.

Sipho shrugged and smiled. Joseph could make his joke if he wanted. He was beginning to understand Joseph.

Sipho asked where the gang had spent the night, and Joseph explained that they had decided to take another chance with the old *pozzie*. But when Sipho asked about Jabu, Joseph turned sullen. At first, all he would say was that Jabu had left.

"Where did he go?" asked Sipho, shocked.

At last he got the story. Jabu had left the gang to go into a shelter for street children. *Malunde* who went there had to promise not to smoke *iglue*, and there were some other rules they had to keep to. They also had to go to school.

"I tried it there once," added Joseph. "But why must someone tell me I can't smoke *iglue*?"

Sipho wanted to know why none of the gang had spoken about the shelter before.

"We like to be free," was Joseph's reply.

"Where is this place?" asked Sipho. "I want to visit Jabu."

Joseph told him in the end. It was on the other side of Hillbrow, and Sipho took a slightly longer route to avoid going past Danny's Den. He didn't want to meet Mr. Danny. Reaching the place Joseph had described, he found a building set back from the road with bright pictures of children painted all over the walls. The words THEMBA SHELTER were painted above. Was this really a Shelter of Hope? The children in the painting looked happy, but they weren't real. The only door he could see in the building looked firmly closed.

Sipho tried the metal gate at the front but found it was locked. He shook and banged on it a few times, but still no one came. When a man in brown uniform and a guard's hat looked out from the next building, he got ready to run. But instead, the guard pointed with his hand that Sipho should go around the back.

Nervously he pushed the gate leading from the back alley to the shelter. The smell of disinfectant hit him as he made his way past some toilets to the main building. It was all so quiet.

Then he remembered what Joseph had said. Of course, all the children, including Jabu, would be in school at this time of day! There were rules here, and there would be adults in charge who saw that they were kept. Suddenly it struck him what Joseph had meant by "We like to be free!" Any adults inside this shelter would want to know who he, Sipho, was. They would ask him why he wasn't in school, and then they would ask about his family . . . Where might those questions lead? He had to get out of here, quick. If he waited outside, he would see Jabu when he came in. Sipho set off back for the gate.

"*Sawubona, mfana!* How are you, my boy?"

The voice was naturally soft and friendly. It was addressed to him and seemed to expect a reply. Could he ignore it? Sipho turned around to see a woman with a kind face. Her dark eyes looked at him, interested. Not piercing and nosy. Her cheeks had the same smooth brown sheen that Ma's skin used to have before she became unwell.

"*Sawubona*, Mama. I'm fine," Sipho replied in a small, tight voice.

19. It's Okay to Cry

XOXOXOX

Would you like some tea?"

When Sipho hesitated, the woman smiled. "We won't eat you, inside! The children call me Sis Pauline. I'm a care worker here."

She seemed so friendly and at ease that Sipho found himself saying yes. He would like some tea. When she asked him his name, he told her.

"It's quiet now because the children are all in school," she explained, as he followed her into the building.

Inside the shelter, Sipho looked around while Sis Pauline boiled the water. Except for an open kitchen in one corner and a couple of small rooms opposite, it was mostly one big, long room with metal bunk beds along each side. Blankets and covers were spread neatly over the beds. Next to them were tall metal cupboards with padlocks. Who kept the keys, Sipho wondered? Were the children worried about having things stolen by each other or by people from outside? As his eyes traveled around, he noticed that some of the windows were broken. Apart from the beds and cupboards, the room was empty, except for a television and a few chairs and tables at one end.

Sis Pauline seemed to pick up on what Sipho was thinking.

"People try to break in here. So we lock up what we can. They even take the mattresses. It's a big problem for us!"

She put a cup of tea down on a table with a plate of buttered bread and a jar of jam. "Help yourself, Sipho!" she said, pulling up a chair next to his.

She let him drink his tea and eat a piece of bread before asking whether he had come to the shelter to look for a place to stay. Almost without thinking he shook his head.

"I was just looking for my friend. His name is Jabu," he said.

Sis Pauline nodded. "Oh, yes. He joined us last week. How did you two come to be friends?"

Her voice and the question seemed so normal. It wasn't like a teacher trying to catch you at something. Sipho relaxed and began to talk about his friendship with Jabu. He spoke about the gang and how he had stayed with them until they had been attacked and thrown into the lake. Little by little, in reply to Sis Pauline's questions, he began to talk about himself. Before he knew it, he had told her about Mr. Danny and running away from him . . . and how he had been chased by the man with a broken bottle and had spent the night cramped in a garbage can.

All the time he was talking, Sis Pauline was quietly nodding and making sympathetic sounds. Then she repeated her earlier question. Did he want to stay in the shelter too? This time Sipho did not shake his head automatically. What should he say? Sis Pauline saw that he was uncertain.

"I can see you need somewhere safe to stay," she said. "But if you want to come here, there are things we need to know . . . about where you come from and why you left your home."

Her voice was still very calm. It wasn't as if she was accusing him or making a threat, but Sipho could feel the panic rising inside him. Sis Pauline must have seen it in his eyes.

"Don't worry," she said. "No one here will force you to go back to your family if things are bad there, but we have to find out what has really happened."

Sipho felt he only half followed what she said next. Something about "misunderstandings." How children sometimes ran away from home because they thought no one loved them. She said something about parents being "under pressure." Sis Pauline used the word "pressure" a lot.

Sometimes, she added, it was possible for children to go back to their families. Sipho felt his heart freeze at these words. He laid his head down on his hands on top of the table. No, no. He didn't want to think about it.

Then he felt Sis Pauline's arm around his shoulder. She was speaking very quietly.

"Have you got a mother, Sipho? Is she alive?"

He managed a nod. But the next question was too much for him.

"Do you think she misses you?"

A huge sob ripped through him, followed by another and another.

He wasn't sure for how long he cried. But Sis Pauline's arm around him helped. When the sobs had calmed, she got up to get some tissues for him from the small corner room. Through the open door he saw a bed and realized that the care workers must sleep in the shelter too.

"It's okay to cry," Sis Pauline comforted him. "When you cry you know what's inside your heart."

She added that he could sleep there for the night. But the following day he would have to tell them everything so they could decide what to do. Sipho wiped his sleeve across his eyes. He needed to speak to Jabu badly. Perhaps Jabu could advise him what to do. He laid his arm and head down again on the table. Clearing away the cup and plate, Sis Pauline left him alone.

The quiet of the shelter broke with a sudden clatter as a group of boys came through the door. Sipho jerked himself up. Jabu was among them, wearing a bright red sweatshirt instead of his usual gray track top. He waved, almost dancing across the room on seeing Sipho.

"*Heyta*, Sipho! Is it you?"

A couple of boys looked interested, but most of the others busied themselves by their beds or clustered around the kitchen.

"What's up with you, *buti*?" Jabu's large, cheeky eyes had a questioning look. Sipho wondered if Jabu could see he had been crying.

"I was looking for you last night," replied Sipho, avoiding the question. "Joseph told me to look here."

"Come. We'll go outside," said Jabu, locking one arm in Sipho's.

Around the side of the shelter, they sat on a slab of concrete. An apartment building towered above them, blocking out the sun.

"Did you see Brother Zack . . . the manager?" asked Jabu. Sipho shook his head.

"He's okay, he's nice."

Jabu continued talking. He had got tired of living on the streets, he said. There was no future in it. When he had met Sis Pauline, she had spoken about the shelter and school. Joseph, of course, had tried to put him off, but he had decided to try it for himself.

"It's the right thing I've done, man. I know it."

But wouldn't the people here want to send him back to his mother if they could find her? Sipho asked.

"They say I won't go back if people are still killing each other there. But they'll look for my ma and tell her I'm safe."

"What about your uncle?"

Sipho remembered very well how Jabu's mother had asked her brother to take him away and look after him. But his aunt had beaten him, and his uncle hadn't stopped her.

"I told them I'll never, never go back to his place."

Sipho hadn't heard Jabu speak quite so fiercely before.

"But you see it's different with me," Sipho began. "My mother . . . she's missing me . . . I'm sure of it." He was forcing himself to say what he was thinking. "It's my stepfather who beats me . . . and my mother . . . she can't do anything."

He paused; and Jabu was quiet too.

"What if my mother wants me back? Will they make me go?" Even Jabu, who usually had something to say, remained silent.

20. Facing Up to Questions

✕✕◆✕◆✕

If Sipho hadn't been so tired after his night in the garbage can, he might have lain awake all night, worrying about how to answer the adults' questions in the morning. Another care worker, *Bra* Elias, gave him the bed above Jabu. It was the first time he had slept so high up, and he would probably also have worried about rolling off in his sleep. For a little while he lay curled up tightly under his cover, aware of the strangeness of the bed and the darkened shelter full of other *malunde*. He had been so absorbed in thinking about his problems that he hadn't begun to talk properly with any of them yet, even when they had been eating their meal together. It helped knowing that Jabu was underneath him now. After *Bra* Elias turned off the light, there was silence inside the shelter. From outside came the constant rumble of traffic and an eerie glow through the windows, which didn't have curtains. A cold draft was blowing through a broken pane of glass near him. Sipho tugged his cover even more closely around him, and before long he was taken over by heavy sleep.

In the morning when Jabu and the others left for school, Sipho remained behind with Sis Pauline to wait for the shelter manager. He was nervous and still unsure of what he would say, even as Brother Zack walked in. A broad smile lifted the manager's cheeks as he greeted them. Tall and thin, he was about the same height and age as Sipho's stepfather, but his voice couldn't have been more different. Like Sis Pauline's, his way of speaking was quiet and friendly. Sitting at the table, Sipho forced himself to glance across into each adult's eyes before making his decision.

Yes, all right. He would trust them. He would tell them everything and let them go and tell his mother that he was safe. Then they could come back and tell him how his mother was . . . and whether the baby had come . . . and whether he had a little brother or a sister. But they would have to explain to his mother that he couldn't ever live with his stepfather. He would just run away again if they forced him.

Once his mind was made up, Sipho found he could answer their questions. He even told them about taking the money from Ma's purse. At the time he had been so angry he hadn't cared about Ma being upset and worried about him disappearing. Now he understood that she couldn't have stopped his stepfather. It wasn't her fault . . . and he wanted to say he was sorry to her—but never, ever, to *him*.

"I'm very proud of you, Sipho. It's hard to say these things."

When Sis Pauline congratulated him, he felt good. Brother Zack explained that he or one of the care workers would visit Sipho's mother. He understood Sipho's feelings about his stepfather. Nothing, he promised, would be decided until they had the full picture. Sometimes people and situations changed. For some children it was possible to go back home and for others not. In the meantime Sipho was welcome to stay at the shelter as long as he kept to the rules.

"Have you taken *iglue*?" asked Brother Zack.

"No, sir . . ."

The words were out of his mouth as quick as water from a tap. Then he hesitated. Could he not be honest?

"Only one or two times, sir . . . when it was very cold." Brother Zack frowned a little but without looking angry.

"Well, we don't allow it. All the boys here know that. And of course we want you to go to school."

Sipho would go to the shelter's own school at first. The teachers there would help him catch up with his work until he was ready for another school. Sipho didn't say anything. He had hated his school in the township. When he couldn't follow what the teacher was saying there, he got into trouble. Worrying so much about being sent home, he hadn't thought to ask Jabu about the school.

There was also something else for Sipho to think about.

"Do you want us to let Mr. Danny know that you are here with us? He could be worried about you." Sis Pauline's voice was calm.

"No, he doesn't care."

Rushing the words, he felt a sudden dash of anger.

"You can't be sure, Sipho. Some people don't always show their true feelings. We can just tell him you're safe. You don't need to see him."

Sipho shrugged, as if to let what she was saying pass. Let them tell Mr. Danny if they wanted to. He was never going back there. At least if they told him, Judy would find out too. He expected that she and Mama Ada would want to know that he was all right.

When their discussion was over, Sis Pauline helped Sipho choose some clothes from a cupboard and showed him a metal tub and soap for washing his dirty clothes. She also pointed out an ironing board and iron, which he hadn't noticed before.

"Everyone must look after their own clothes. Even if clothes are old they can still be smart," she said, her eyes wrinkling with a smile.

Later, bending over the tub and scrubbing the dirt from his jeans, Sipho pictured Gogo and then Ma doing the same job he was doing now. Their hands and arms covered with soapsuds, their faces shining with sweat. They had always washed his clothes. Even at Mr. Danny's, Mama Ada had done it for him. This was the first time he was doing it himself. Hanging the dripping clothes on the line outside the shelter, he felt a little bit proud of his work. What would Ma think if she could see him now?

In the middle of the afternoon, like the day before, the quiet of the shelter was broken when Jabu and the other boys returned from the school. But this time, Sipho took more in. There were quite a few faces he had seen before in the video games shop. Some children were smaller than him, and others looked much older. This was the group that went to the shelter school, explained Jabu. The boys who came in a little later, wearing gray trousers and maroon or black blazers, were those attending schools in the city or Soweto.

A boy with closely cropped hair called out to Jabu. "Does your friend want to play?"

He was holding up a pack of cards. Sipho

wondered if his head had been shaved like Joseph's. Jabu looked at Sipho, and they joined the cardplayers at the table. With the television blaring out loudly behind them, Sipho turned his chair sideways so from time to time he could glance at the screen. Some boys were playing with a ball in the middle of the room, while a couple of the older ones had set up desks for themselves by pulling tables in between the beds. Somehow they were managing to work despite all the noise. The night before, Sis Pauline and *Bra* Elias had insisted on a quiet time for homework after they had eaten. These students must have a lot to do if that time wasn't enough.

"Do the teachers shout at you at this school?" Sipho asked, as Jabu dealt the cards.

The boy with the nearly shaved head answered first. "Today I was looking out of the window and Mr. Peters shouted at me because I wasn't working."

"But they help you more. There are not so many children here," said Jabu.

In the morning Sipho was taken in a van with the others to an old house in a nearby suburb. There was no sign saying it was a school. *Bra* Elias took Sipho to the office. The head teacher, a small man with bright, dancing eyes, shook Sipho's hand before asking him to sit down. "I'm

Mr. Masango. I don't know why, but everyone just calls me Mr. M.! Hehe!"

He chuckled, as if this was a special joke, before beginning his questions. Had Sipho been to school before? Where was his school? What standards did he pass? What was his best subject? With each new question, Sipho's stomach became tighter and his voice smaller and fainter. He couldn't tell this head teacher that he didn't have a "best subject." Or that school to him meant being hit and called "stupid." Then suddenly Mr. M. jumped up from his chair and asked Sipho to come with him. It was like trying to follow a rock rabbit! Mr. M. darted up the stairs with Sipho struggling to keep up with him.

Flinging open a door, the head teacher signaled for Sipho to step inside. Eyes down, Sipho entered the room.

"Teacher Lindi, here is your new student. His name is Sipho, and I know he is going to be a star!"

There was laughter. But it didn't sound unkind.

"Hello, Sipho. Have you any friends here?" asked the teacher.

Her voice was firm but welcoming. Sipho looked up, and there was Jabu! There were only four others. In his township class he had been one of seventy!

"Yes, Teacher. He's my friend," he whispered, pointing at Jabu.

"Then you can sit next to him. So long as you work hard and don't chat all day!"

"Oh, I'm sure they won't do that, Teacher Lindi!" Mr. M. announced as if he was talking to a large crowd. "I know all you boys are going to work hard and be superstars!"

Again there were smiles and giggles as he slipped out of the room. Is this really a school? thought Sipho.

21. Rubble and Ash

M any things were new and strange to Sipho at the shelter school. Like lessons in "Drama," where Teacher Lindi asked him to imagine someone who was lonely and make up a scene about it with the other boys. Like a teacher sitting next to him and talking with him when he had a problem with his work. Like Teacher Joe, who was white, with long reddish hair hanging from the back of his head like a horse's tail. His pink face was covered in little brown dots, and he wore bright shirts. At the end of Sipho's first art lesson, Teacher Joe praised Sipho's painting.

"I like the way you use your colors, Sipho. They're bold and strong. That's good!"

But Sipho felt wary. Teacher Joe seemed friendly, but so had Mr. Danny.

Soon Sipho found he was beginning to enjoy some lessons. Even math and English weren't so bad. In fact, sometimes the subjects were all mixed up. He especially liked the work for the

Peace Day that Teacher Lindi had told them about. They were using a sewing machine to make a banner. Having measured and cut out the letters for the word PEACE from some blue material, they were stitching them onto a long strip of white. Sipho was asked to trace a picture of a dove so they could have it flying on the banner. There were also songs to learn. While some of the English words were difficult, others made sense to him:

Sister, brother,
Mamma, daddy,
Stop killing one another
Bring peace in our Land.

Teacher Lindi joined in the singing. Her voice seemed to come from deep inside her, encouraging them to sing more loudly. Her slim black braids, pulled back together into a thick bunch, swung as she moved with the music. On the following Sunday, thousands of children were going to join hands in one enormous circle around the city center to sing their Peace Song. Then they would go in buses to a very big meeting especially for children.

"Is it for all children, Teacher?" asked Jabu.
"Do you mean is it for black and white?"
Jabu nodded.

"It is," replied Teacher Lindi. "Look how the song says 'Let's bury our differences and live in harmony.' That means we must learn to live together in peace."

Yes, thought Sipho. But who would listen to children singing a song?

Of all his lessons, Sipho soon found he was looking forward most of all to art. Teacher Joe said they should make pictures of a time when they had felt really sad or happy or angry or frightened or whatever else. He said a picture could show how someone felt without any words. Most times, Sipho would sit at the table thinking, and then the picture would just come to him. First he drew himself hiding in the garbage can and the man with the broken bottle standing over him. He made himself very small and the man very big. Then he made a picture of himself playing with his puppy in Gogo's yard. The puppy's tail stuck straight up in the air! He painted the gang eating Vusi's sausages around the fire at the *pozzie*.

When Jabu looked at this picture, he laughed at the way Sipho had given each *malunde* a round, fat stomach to show how they enjoyed their meal! But another picture showed *malunde* tightly packed inside the back of a *gumba-gumba*, holding on to each other. He made black dots to show tears dripping out of their eyes.

There were two things, however, which Sipho

found it hard to bring himself to draw. Anything that had to do with his mother was still too upsetting. The other had to do with Mr. Danny. There were so many different sides to Mr. Danny, and Sipho's feelings about him and his family were so mixed up, it was too confusing. In the end Teacher Joe helped with a suggestion.

"When you don't know what to do, stop thinking so much. Just let your hand draw whatever it wants. It'll know what to do!"

Giving Sipho a large piece of paper, he told him he could put a lot of different pictures and ideas on it.

Sipho began drawing in the top left-hand corner and then adding more drawings around the page, but leaving it blank in the middle. He drew himself cozy in bed, Copper the dog nuzzling his hand, himself playing cards with Judy and Portia, Mama Ada carrying a plate of sizzling chicken. Then he drew a tall man with a mustache pointing a finger at a little figure with a broom. Another drawing showed Mr. Danny pointing to a big clock and himself holding up T-shirts to people passing by. The pockets of his trousers were hanging out to show he had no money. Another picture showed two boys facing each other. The boy David had sharp, hateful lines coming out of his eyes, and out of his mouth came the word THIEF.

When the page was filled up except for the space in the middle, he suddenly knew what to do. First he drew a large metal gate. On one side he drew a house and on the other side a long road. Then he drew two boys looking at each other, one on each side of the gate. Their eyes were large and sad. Under the boy by the house he wrote SIPHO, and under the other he wrote JABU. Teacher Joe came to look.

"Mmmmm," he said, staring at the picture for quite a long time. "You have said a lot in this, Sipho. Well done."

It was a couple of weeks after Sipho's arrival at the shelter that Brother Zack called him aside. The lines on his forehead seemed deeper than usual, and his eyes were grave. He had gone to look for Sipho's mother, using the directions Sipho had given him. But instead of the rows of homemade shacks that Sipho had described, he had found a wide stretch of rubble and ash.

He had gone to the nearest house. The people there told him that there had been fighting after someone from the men's hostel had been stabbed. The hostel dwellers believed the murderer came from the shacks and had set out to take their revenge with fire. The police were called, but it was the usual story. Taking their time, they came too late to stop the men from the hostels. The fire spread so quickly that people had run from their homes with only time to save themselves. Later some of them had returned to collect whatever hadn't been eaten up by the fire.

Sipho's mouth felt dry. He couldn't speak. His mind was exploding. He could see fire licking up the curtains by Ma's bed, flaring over the bed-covers, curling around his mattress, the card-board boxes, the table . . . Smoke billowing out so you couldn't see anything anymore. But where in all this was Ma? Had she got off her bed in time? Or was she moving so heavily that she couldn't get to the door? Or had she stopped to grab out of the flames a small, crying bundle wrapped in a shawl?

"I feel sure your mother will be all right." Brother Zack was talking, but his words hardly made sense. "They told me that many people escaped the fire."

Sipho forced himself to speak. "But where did they go?"

"That's what I shall find out, Sipho. Don't be too worried. We are going to find your mother."

Putting his arm around Sipho, Brother Zack held him firmly for a few seconds and then asked Sipho to think if there were any relatives or friends who might have helped his mother. He would go and see them and he would also contact priests and other people who worked in the community. Someone was bound to know.

That evening Sipho didn't want to eat. After Brother Zack had spoken to him, he lay on his bed and refused to come down. He didn't even want to talk to Jabu. The next day was Saturday, and although Sipho did his share of the chores, he again refused to join in the activities. The others were going to play soccer against a team from a school in the suburbs. They were going to be taken in that school's bus to their soccer field. Sipho had heard the talk about the enormous fields belonging to the school and how the students there even had their own sports center. In the township they played soccer in the road.

Jabu tried to persuade him.

"Come on, *buti*! You'll feel better when you get out."

But Sipho was adamant. He was not going anywhere. In the end, Sis Pauline agreed that he could stay behind.

"I'm going to make some badges for the Peace Day tomorrow. You'll help me, won't you, Sipho?" she said.

He didn't say anything. It would be hard to say no to Sis Pauline.

But the Peace Day and the rally no longer attracted him. He had thought it would be good, singing with lots of other young people in the streets. Now he was confused. Peace was good. Yes, he wanted peace. But when he thought about the men from the hostel setting fire to Ma's home, he felt so angry. Like he was burning inside himself. Ma had never hurt them. Why shouldn't their homes be burned down as well? Another wild thought had also crept into his head. If his stepfather had been caught inside the burning shack instead of his mother, then he wouldn't be upset.

Sitting next to Sis Pauline, Sipho helped her cut the white and blue ribbons before twisting and pinning them together. She let him work in silence. He liked her for that. Afterward he helped her make sandwiches, which she said they would take with them to eat during the rally. Sis Pauline seemed to think of everything. Perhaps he would just go with everyone else, but no one . . . no one could force him to sing.

22. "We Are the Future . . ."

❖❖❖❖❖

We are the future, the core of this land . . ."

Voices rose up all around Sipho. The long line of young people linking hands stretched down the hill as far as he could see. As Teacher Lindi had told them, black and white children had come together. Blues and whites shimmered everywhere in the sunlight, standing out front all the other colors. White doves circled in blue on caps, shirts, banners and badges. Even the sky seemed dressed in the colors of peace. White clouds against a blue sky.

Sipho was linking hands in between Jabu and Teacher Lindi. The teachers from school had come to the shelter, and they had all walked together to join the route for the Peace Link. In fact it was more of a jog than a walk as they kept pace with Mr. M. People in the streets had stared at them carrying their banner declaring PEACE and wearing their blue and white ribbon badges. Some had waved, some had even called out to support them. Only a few had given them nasty looks. When one passerby made a rude comment loud enough for them to hear, Jabu had quickly retorted, "No polecat ever knew its own smell!"

"So even polecats must learn to make a fresh start in the new South Africa, hey, Jabu!" Teacher Joe had laughed.

Even though he wasn't singing now as he stood between Jabu and Teacher Lindi, it was difficult for Sipho not to feel some of the excitement. Then a word in the song jolted him again.

Look around, link your hands
Feel the peace flowing out
Feel the love burning again . . .

Burning. Blues and whites were once more wiped out by a picture of fire. Red, gray and black. Flames, smoke and ash. How could he sing this song? And yet Jabu was singing. His mother was probably also burned out of her home. Didn't that make him angry and make him want to do something back to the attackers? But that meant the killing would go on for ever.

Teacher Lindi's hand pressed more tightly on his as her voice rose up even more strongly with the last lines of the song.

We will give everything
To see everyone stand hand in hand.

The words echoed in the silence that fol- lowed. Most people lowered their heads. Sipho dropped his too, although it was no good trying to pray. What was the point when bad things kept happening all the time? But if he could have a wish or a prayer come true, it would be that Ma and the baby were all right.

Later, at the stadium, Sipho thought he had never seen so many young people in one place. Speeches rang out over a loudspeaker.

"Young people must tell adults that they have had enough of hate and violence . . ."

People cheered.

"The youth must speak out and let their voices be heard . . ."

The cheering continued.

"Now is the time to look forward. We want a future!" The audience broke into song.

South Africa, we love you,
Our beautiful land . . .

Bodies moved in waves to the music. It was impossible not to be caught up in it. Jabu grinned when he saw Sipho relax a little. "Let's look around," he suggested.

Slipping away from the others, they began to squeeze their way through the crowd at the bottom of the stands. Jabu headed toward the raised platform for the speakers and singers.

"I want to see what this deejay looks like!"

They were almost out of the crush of people when Sipho heard someone call his name. Looking around, he couldn't see who it was and thought it must have been a mistake. But then it came again, and this time the voice sounded familiar. A girl's voice.

"Sipho, please wait! We're coming!"

It sounded just like Judy. Was she here? He scanned the crowd but couldn't see her. There were so many people. Jabu was already somewhere ahead. Sipho wasn't sure he wanted to see her.

But before he had time to decide whether to slip away or stay, there was Judy in front of him, and close behind her was Portia, edging their way through the bustle of people. Judy with her head crisscrossed with long corn-colored plaits, woven with blue and white beads, matching Portia's style. Both girls looked really pleased to see him.

"I'm so happy to see you, Sipho. How're you keeping?" Judy's voice was rapid, slightly out of breath and anxious.

"It's fine with me," he replied. He knew he wasn't smiling.

"Judy was really worried when you left," added Portia.

"You shouldn't have let David get to you like that." Judy spoke forcefully. "It was a horrid little note. He admitted to it after you'd gone. Dad was really mad at him."

But it wasn't just the note. It wasn't just David. Couldn't she see that? Sipho looked away. How could he explain? He should leave, find Jabu and avoid this conversation.

"Your dad confuses me sometimes, too." Portia spoke softly.

It was noisy, but he was sure he had heard correctly, and a question suddenly occurred to him that he hadn't thought about before. Portia had always seemed to be enjoying her time with Judy. But what was it like for her in Mr. Danny's house? Did Mr. Danny and David sometimes say things that made her feel uncomfortable too . . . even though she was Judy's best friend? He saw Judy turn to look at Portia as if there was a question she needed to ask her.

They were interrupted by a blast of music and Jabu reappearing through the crowd.

"Come on, man! Oh . . ." Jabu stopped when he saw the girls. "Won't you introduce me?"

The girls laughed, and Sipho told them his friend's name.

"Hi, Jabu!" Judy and Portia spoke together.

"Did you two come on your own or are you in a group?" asked Portia, her eyes traveling between the two of them.

Sipho explained that they had come with others from the Themba Shelter.

"That's not far from Hillbrow, is it? You should at least come and visit us sometime, Sipho. I would really like that, and I know Ada would like to see you too. She was very worried about you." Her voice was so earnest. Glancing at Jabu, she added, "You could bring your friend too."

"Sure!" Jabu grinned.

But Sipho could feel his stomach knotting up. Did Judy understand so little about why he had left?

"Jabu was at your house one time but he never came in," Sipho replied.

"Why not?" Judy's blue eyes looked troubled.

He was tempted just to shrug and not bother explaining. Surely she could work it out for herself? Instead he answered sharply, "Talk to your father and your brother."

Judy's face turned deep pink. "You sound so angry with me, Sipho . . . I'm really sorry about what happened. You know I argue with Dad and David when I think they're wrong . . . but I can't help what they think!"

"Hey, cool it, *buti*! You're giving this girl a hard time," Jabu interrupted. "Today we're talking love and peace, man! Leave all that other stuff for another day."

As if Jabu's words had been heard, a voice over the loudspeaker called for everyone to come down from the stands into the field and to link hands for a final song. In the surge forward, Sipho found himself between Portia and Judy in a line of people snaking their way across the field. A clutch of blue balloons with white doves flew upward above them, together at first and then whirling away in different directions. Sipho's arms were swinging with everyone else's to the rhythm, and on each side he could hear Judy's and Portia's voices ringing out.

Forget about the past
And build a new nation.

How could he forget what had happened to him? Bad things were still happening. He could hear a voice in his head saying that he didn't believe these words. But when the song came to the final verse, the voice in his head was quiet. If only these words could be true.

Sister, brother,
Mamma, daddy,
Stop killing one another
Bring peace in our Land.

23. Dreams

❊❖❊❖❊❖❊

Seated between Sis Pauline and a young woman with a baby, Sipho strained to see out of the taxi's dusty windows. The minibus was jolting over the potholes in the road. Every sharp knock made the baby bump on its mother's lap. In between the bumps, the small face, with large eyes and plump, shiny cheeks, stared at Sipho. As the driver took a corner too quickly, Sipho's hand shot out and the baby grabbed hold of his finger.

"She likes you," laughed the mother.

"Your little sister will soon be big like this one," added Sis Pauline.

The baby shifted its serious eyes to Sis Pauline and back to Sipho, still holding tightly to his finger. Then her mouth broke into a smile, showing two small, white teeth. Despite the tightness in his stomach, he gave her a quick smile and turned again to look beyond the glass. It seemed such a long time ago that he had been in a taxi going the other way. He remembered how his heart had been thumping wildly that day he was escaping. It was beginning to do the same thing now that he was coming back. He couldn't help feeling excited about seeing Ma and the baby. But would Ma still be angry? What would she say to him? And could he be sure that the person he feared most would be out of the way?

"Your stepfather won't be there. Your mother promised me that. You can go when he's not around. She's crying to see you."

Those had been Brother Zack's exact words when he came to tell Sipho that he had found his mother. It was a priest who knew where to find Ma. As soon as Brother Zack spoke about a pregnant woman, the priest knew who it was. On the night of the burning, people had run to his church for safety. Ma's pains had begun that night, and the priest had driven her to the hospital himself. A member of his church agreed to let Ma and her baby stay for a while in a shed in their backyard. But there were problems. Even though the shed was tiny, Sipho's stepfather insisted he must stay there too. There had been arguments with the people in the house, and they wanted Ma to find another place.

Outside, the sight of houses with charred bricks, no roofs, no windows, startled Sipho. Had the fighting with the men from the hostels reached this far? The taxi wouldn't go past the men's hostel, or past the place deep inside the township where Ma had lived before. Taxi drivers kept to the roads that were supposed to be safer. But it seemed nowhere was safe. Nowhere.

The taxi juddered to a halt opposite a line of shops. Windows were boarded up, others were covered by heavy metal grilles, and paint was peeling off the walls. A layer of dust covered the pavement and the steps leading into the shops.

"We must walk from here," said Sis Pauline.

At the corner, a group of young men playing cards stopped to look at them. Farther down the road some small children chasing a wheel with a stick almost ran into Sipho. Even in the middle of the week, there were a lot of people around. All those without jobs in the city. Sipho nervously scanned the figures in the road ahead. Ma had told Brother Zack that his stepfather would be out. But what if they met him on the way? Sis Pauline couldn't protect him. Ma hadn't been able to. Maybe his stepfather wouldn't grab him in the middle of the street, but Sipho wouldn't wait to find out. He would just have to run like he had never run before.

Behind the wire fence and gate of Number 153 stood a small redbrick house, a shade deeper than the dry red earth all around it.

"We should greet the people in the house

first before we go to the back," whispered Sis Pauline, leading Sipho to the front door.

When no one replied to their knocking, they made their way around the side of the house. In the next yard, a lady hanging out clothes stopped to greet them. Two small children ran from behind her up to the fence to stare at Sipho.

"We've come to visit the lady who lives at the back here," Sis Pauline explained.

"*Kulungile*, Mama . . . that's good. She's inside with the baby." She pointed across to a small shed made of corrugated iron. A washing line crossed the yard from a bare tree to the corner of the house. Wet squares of white cotton and a couple of tiny undershirts caught the brightness of the sunlight. An iron tub, full of water, stood near the shed, and damp patches on the dry earth showed that it wasn't long since Ma had been washing.

"Who is the young man?" asked the neighbor, looking at Sipho.

"This is her son," replied Sis Pauline.

Before the neighbor could reply, the shed door rattled, opening noisily. Ma stepped out, a baby wrapped in a white shawl in her arms.

Seeing her face light up, Sipho wanted to dash across to her and feel her arm around him, but he held back, uncertain what to do. Instead he kept beside Sis Pauline, both of them lowering their heads under the washing to get to Ma, who was greeting them.

"It's many weeks since I have seen you, my son. I think you are taller now."

Her face looked strained, but she was smiling. Her eyes seemed to be calling him, and he was sure that she would hug him if he went closer, but he still held back awkwardly. Wiping his sleeve across his face, he looked down at the ground while Sis Pauline introduced herself.

They followed Ma into the shed. It was half the size of the shack where they had lived before. At the back was a single mattress on the floor and in front some wooden crates. On one of them stood a kerosene stove with a single pot, a couple of plates and mugs stacked underneath. A small bag of *mealie* meal and a few other packages were piled in one corner. There was hardly room for the three of them to stand. Ma left the door open, which let in the only light apart from a small window at the side.

"Sit on the mattress and you can hold your sister."

Gently Ma lowered the baby. She and Sis Pauline each sat on a crate. Making a cradle with his arms against his knees, he looked down at the little face, the tiny eyelids and lips twitching in sleep.

"What's her name, Ma?"

"It's Thembi. For me she is 'hope.' You ran away and left me, my son."

Ma's voice trembled, and Sipho did not know what to say. It was true.

"When I gave you the name of Sipho, it was because you were a 'gift' to me. I didn't know I would lose my gift. Now I know. With children, we can only hope."

"It's very true what you say, Mama," Sis Pauline agreed.

"That is why we call our shelter 'Themba.' It's a place of hope."

For a while Sipho listened as the two women spoke, at the same time watching little Thembi sleeping. Every now and again he stroked her head lightly and waited to see if any part of her would move. He was hoping she would wake up so she would look at him too. When Sis Pauline began talking about *malunde*, Sipho was slowly encouraged to join in and tell Ma bits and pieces about how he had been living. He began to relax, and when Ma boiled water in the pot for some tea, she insisted Sipho drink his before she used the same mug for herself. However, there were things he did not tell Ma. He didn't mention *iglue*, and he said nothing about being attacked, the *gumba-gumba*, the lake or the man with the broken bottle.

"Is it true, my son, that you stayed with a

white family?" Brother Zack must have said something about Mr. Danny.

"I was working in the shop, Ma, and the owner, Mr. Danny, took me home . . . but his son didn't like it. Only the daughter . . . she was friendly."

"I see you have been learning many things," Ma said quietly.

There was sadness in Ma's eyes. She said nothing about him stealing money from her purse. Nothing about him running away. If she was still angry with him, he had to know.

"I'm sorry I took your money, Ma . . . I didn't have money for the taxi . . . I had to get away from him, Ma . . ."

It was out . . . from his own mouth. Would Ma lecture him now about his stepfather? He didn't think he could take it. But with the baby sleeping in his arms, he couldn't just jump up and storm out. He took a deep breath and waited to hear what Ma would say.

Sis Pauline spoke first.

"Many *malunde* run away because there's trouble with a stepfather. It's so common, especially when the stepfather is under pressure . . . like no job and no money."

There was silence. Sipho bit his lip and looked at Ma. To his surprise and dismay, a tear was rolling down her cheek.

"I felt so bad when he ran away. It was like I had forced away my own child . . . because this husband of mine was always angry with him . . . and I couldn't stop this man . . ."

Ma's voice was choked. Sis Pauline took Ma's hands in hers.

"Don't be upset with yourself, my sister. Life is hard and we all have to learn how to live it."

Sipho sat softly rocking the baby, trying to take in what Ma had said. She wasn't angry with him. She was blaming herself. He himself had blamed her for letting his stepfather beat him, never thinking how hard it had been for her too. Ma was now explaining to Sis Pauline that his stepfather was trying to get a job. There was a rumor that some men were needed for road work. That was where he was today. If only he could start earning, she felt sure he would become calmer and change back to how he had been when she first met him. Then they could rent a proper house with enough rooms for them all, and perhaps . . .

Ma didn't finish her sentence. Sipho had declared he would never go back while his stepfather was there. Brother Zack must have told her that. What Ma was saying was surely just a dream.

"I understand your feelings, Mama," said Sis Pauline, "and I can see that you are praying for your husband to change. But will he do something about his drinking problem?"

Suddenly Ma was downcast again.

"You want Sipho to come home, Mama, and we want him to be with you too. But he can't come home while your husband is drinking and then beating him. He'll just run away again."

"I hear what you are saying," Ma said quietly.

Sipho listened intently as the two women spoke. He could see what Sis Pauline was doing. She was saying to Ma very gently that Ma mustn't build all her hopes on his stepfather changing . . . that if she wanted Sipho to return, she must be able to offer him a safe home. Baby Thembi needed a safe home too. Sis Pauline was actually asking Ma to think about what she herself could do to change things. What Judy had once told him about Mama Ada flashed through his mind . . . that she had got rid of her husband, who was always drinking. Mama Ada seemed such a strong and wise person. But maybe she too had once been like Ma.

"Give us a chance to work with you," Sis Pauline was saying. "We can keep Sipho for a little while to give you time to work things out. We're not God, Mama, but we can try to help you. Women have to learn to be very strong."

Baby Thembi's eyelids fluttered and opened.

She lay looking up at Sipho with big, trusting eyes.

"*Sawubona*, Thembi! Hello, my little sister! Let me see you now you are awake."

Sipho lifted her up to face him, putting his hand behind her wobbly head. She felt so firm and delicate at the same time.

"See how she's looking at you!" laughed Sis Pauline. "When she's a bit older, she won't let you go."

For a few minutes Sis Pauline and Ma sat talking about babies while Sipho and Thembi continued to examine each other. Then Sis Pauline stood up.

"It's time for us to get back now, Mama. You have our phone number. Just ring me or Brother Zack any time you want."

With Thembi wrapped on her back, Ma walked with them. Outside the shops, a taxi was filling up with passengers.

"*Sala kahle*, Mama." Sis Pauline shook Ma's hand. "We'll try to look after your son well."

"Will you come to see me and your sister, Sipho?"

Ma's voice was strange, and her eyes were wet. She was trying to hold back her tears. Throwing his arms around her, he held her tightly. Ma's arms enclosed him. He could feel sobs rising inside him. Swallowing hard, he pushed them back down. Releasing himself, he promised to come again.

"I want to bring Thembi a present, Ma," he said, but he didn't say what it was.

By saving up the pocket money Brother Zack gave out on Fridays, he was going to buy the little wooden rhino. It would be his own special gift to his sister. When she learned to sit up like the baby in the taxi, she would be able to hold it in her fist, and Ma could make up little stories, like Gogo used to do when he was small.

From the back window of the taxi, Sipho watched as Ma waved, getting smaller and smaller. He waved back until she was only a speck. Turning around, he pressed his lips tightly together, aware that other passengers were looking. But Sis Pauline took no notice of them. Putting her arm around his shoulders, she hugged him. He remembered what she had said before. It's okay to cry . . . and when you cry you know what is inside your heart. Sipho's eyes filled up. Ma had her dreams, and so did he. If only she could be strong . . . like Mama Ada. But if her dreams didn't come true, then perhaps his would. If he did well in school, one day he would get a job and a house. Ma and Thembi could stay with him then. They were part of his dream . . . Sipho let the tears flow.

Glossary

amatrolley: (mixture of Zulu and English) shopping cart(s)

baasie: (Afrikaans) little boss

baba: (Zulu) father

bafana: (Zulu) boys

bhiyo: (based on the American word "bioscope") movie theater

bra: (slang) brother

buti: (Afrikaans) brother; here it is used like "pal"

cha!: (Zulu) no!

cheesekop: (mixture of English and Afrikaans) "cheese-head"; used as an insult

gumba-gumba: (from the Zulu word "umgumba," the swooping tail of a bird) a large police van

hamba kahle: (Zulu; "k" pronounced as "g") go well or good-bye

hawu!: (Zulu) expression of shock or surprise

hayi!: (Zulu) no!

heyta!: hi!

iglue: (based on the English word "glue") glue

Ja: (Afrikaans; pronounced "ya") yes

Jabu: ("j" pronounced as in English; "injabulo" in
    Zulu) joy
kulungile: (Zulu) "it's good"
magents: (slang) gentlemen
malunde: (Zulu slang) a person living on the street
Matomatoes: (slang) the man with the red face
mbamba: (Zulu) beer
mealie meal: cornmeal, which is made into porridge
mealies: (from Afrikaans *"mielie"*) corn
mfana: (Zulu) boy
pozzie: (slang) a safe place or hideout
rand: 1 rand = 100 cents
sala kahle: (Zulu "k" pronounced as "g") stay well or
    good-bye
sawubona: (Zulu) greetings—day or night
scheme: (slang) gang
shesha!: (Zulu) hurry up!
Sipho: (pronounced "Seepo"; "isipho" in Zulu) gift
stompie: (Afrikaans) cigarette end or stump
takkies: gym shoes or running shoes
Themba: (pronounced "Temba"; "ithemba" in Zulu)
    trust or hope
tiekie-dice: (mixture of Afrikaans and English) a gam-
    bling game using small change and two dice
tsotsi: (Sotho) a gangster or thug
umlungu: (Zulu) a white person
umrabaraba: (Zulu) a game like checkers

vuilgoed: (Afrikaans; "v" pronounced as "f," "g" hard
     and guttural) dirty rubbish
we bafana!: (Zulu) you boys!
yebo: (Zulu) yes

Pronunciation of Zulu vowels
A as in "ark"
E as in "bed"
I as in "ease"
O as in "ore"
U as in "pool"

About the Author

For many years South Africa was the most openly racist country in the world. Beverley Naidoo learned about it not only as a white child with privilege, but later as a student who joined the active resistance to apartheid. In exile in England, Beverley wrote her first children's book, *Journey to Jo'burg: A South African Story*, in 1985. Although banned in South Africa until 1991, this enormously successful book helped hundreds of thousands of young readers elsewhere to understand what life under apartheid meant for children. A sequel, *Chain of Fire*, followed her young characters as they tried to resist the government's bulldozing their homes and forcing them to move to a "homeland."